THE BOOK OF DAVID

THE BOOK OF DAVID

God, Life, and Recovery

David O'Meara

Rev. date: 09/03/2019

To order additional copies of this book, contact:
Xlibris
1-888-795-4274
www.Xlibris.com
Orders@Xlibris.com
802388

CONTENTS

INTRODUCTION

My name is David A. O'Meara. I was born in August of 1983, in a hospital in Okinawa, Japan. My Father (Brian) and Mother (Kathy) lived in military housing in Japan with my three brothers (Brian, Mike, and Kevin) and my sister (Erin). We are the O'Meara's.

But my book goes into my personal struggles with my drug addiction. My struggles with mental health. And my relationship with Jesus.

I started drinking when I was 11 years old, sneaking bears from my friend's father's stash. It escalated into other drugs.

I was diagnosed with Schizophrenia and depression when I was 27. I spent time in the mental hospital and am still in counseling and seeing a psychiatrist.

A veteran, I joined the military in May of 2008. Later I received an honorable discharge from the military for medical reasons.

This is a book about my feelings, my dreams, and different points of view of my experiences through these times. I hope to touch people through my life experiences

So sit back and enjoy the ride. For this is the Book of David: God, Life, and Recovery.

BOOK ONE

DREAMS

I went to bed
Feeling great
When I was sleeping
I had a bad dream
I had a dream
I had killed my younger brother
It started out we were talking
I pulled out a knife
And stabbed him
Over and over again
I sat there and laughed so hard
then I said don't fuck with me
You little fuckin shit
I sat there and watched him die
There on the dirt
I didn't care
I just walked away
I left him for dead
In the middle of the desert
I woke up and I was crying
Because I had killed someone
I love so much
I sat there thinking about this dream
It scared the shit out of me
These are the kind of dreams
I have every day
Dreams of murder
Why, I do not know
But there is nothing
About the dreams I have

SLEIGHT

What is all this we can not fathom
Is it the truth told in sleight lies so seldom
Is this life wrapped up in a situation
Is this me getting caught up in life's fixations
What is this that eats at my soul
Will this consume the world as a whole
What will come, what will be seen
Will this shit ever end
Is this all the things that have been
Mixing all together into one big blend
What is this big thing called life
Will I act out with strife
Will I get caught up in the whirlwind
Will I get caught up in sin

VIOLENCE IN THE WORLD

Why can't you see
Through anything
If you look deep into this world
It is full of hate, rage and murder
We are killing each other off
For no reason at all
Why do we kill
There is no reason for it
I used to feel these things
In my life
When I got fucked up
I would reach out with strife
And let my anger roam free
I wish the world
To be a better place
Of peace and honesty
This will never happen
There is too much hate in the world
We have been at war
From the beginning
And there will be till the end
Why are there such things
As terrorism
All throughout the world
You can kill their leader
And they continue to fight till the end

Why are there gangs
They shouldn't exist
You are wearing gang colors
Bang you're dead
That person dies for no reason
Just for wearing gang colors
I will steal from you
I will sell you drugs
I will kill you
If you try to stop me
As you can see
There is too much violence
In this world we live in

SILENCE

I will not talk
I will stay quiet
I will sit in the dark
So no one will talk to me
There are so many secrets
I choose to hold inside
So I sit by myself
In Isolation
I am depressed
Because I keep silent
I don't care
Because I don't want the consequences
If I tell I could die
My friends would consider me a narc
So I shut the fuck up
And don't say a word
This way I hold so much in
I am scared for my life
So I shut my mouth
This is why I keep secrets
And choose to keep silent
Because I am scared for my life

MY INNER VOICE

My inner voice tells me what to do
It takes me places I don't want to be
I am at war everyday
With that voice in my head
It could lead me to my death
Or it can lead me the right way
I am struggling with that voice in my head
It is telling me to go out and get high
I am scared of the voice sometimes
Because sometimes it tells me to kill
I fight so I won't go out and kill
I lived a hard life of
Physical and sexual abuse
My inner voice knows this
And it uses it against me
It rips me apart inside
I don't like my inner self
So I go nuts because of
All the shit in my head
In the end I wish I was dead
So fuck you
That voice inside of me
I will not give you
No more sympathy
So fuck you and go away

PEEK HOLE

Eyes are open
I see deception in the worldly life
Spirit racing
To find the holy one
I stand before you on Holy ground
Your will revealed
As I ask out loud
You listen closely to my prayers
I hear a gentle whisper in my ears
As you speak fear overcomes me
Satan tempting to lead me astray
The battle for good and bad
Goes on inside me
I use the weapon God wove inside my body
I hang my flesh on the cross daily
Your will be done, not mine
What you reveal is a blessing
Even if it leads to pain and trials
For what is bad in my eyes
Might be meant for good in the path ahead
My eyes are open wider now
But still it is hard to see
I see you a little bit more
Everyday I live for you
Simple-minded people living all around me
Allowing me to see
What I need to work on inside myself
You put them there for a purpose
To change who we are
We are pure in spirit
But our hearts wicked
God's spirit inside of us
Allows us to repent from the past
Forgiveness brings love
Unforgiveness brings hate

The spirit inside tells us
To have faith, hope, and to love
Our flesh is trying to tell us different
But to know He is really there
Is all the comfort I need?
Cause I know
And I see that He is protecting me
Cause I am alive today
I see the spiritual realm a little bit
But I see it as if I am looking through
A peek hole

MESSED UP WORLD

What is the simplicity of things that are here.
Are they the things that change who we are?
Do they draw us nearer to who we are?
These are simple questions
Which we ask ourselves.
Life is simpler than it may seem
If we trust in ourselves.
What are the worries of this world
That hold us back?
What do you see
When you look at humanity and its flaws?
Is there a chance for humanity
And the things that keep us going?
Does the world spin
And we stick to the ground?
Do we see that if the world stopped spinning
Would we float and have no gravity?
Is humanity finished
Or will we persevere through everything?
Life is a gift and we shall live on.
What do we do for change in the world?
What does it mean
When it feels like your world is upside down?
Does is mean your world is in a mess?
Welcome to the world of humanity,
Which is one big mess.

FREEDOM

Gray clouds fill the sky
Over the green brush and dirt of the earth
Consumed in the thoughts of nature
Bring positivity to what was once negative
I sit and think about the freedom of my mind
Brought to me by a peace of others
And looking out upon the earth
And reflecting
On what is good about the world
Snow the symbolism of purity,
And oxidizing air,
And life
Bring me to a state of wonder and peace
It is as if time stops for a second
For my life to restart and move on
To the better things of life
I remember the good times today
And not the bad
Man isn't it a blessing?
I love it.
Let my mind remain in peace
One day at a time
I see a picture of peace before my eyes
And it is not framed
Because it is not entrapped
But it is free
From the things that keep it bound
Breaking the chains of hellish torment
Of prison

HOLD ON

There is a complacency
That lies within my dark soul
Eaten alive by what is
Is this a disease
That eats away at mankind
Or is this just a part of my imagination
Consuming me to the brink of insanity
Compelling me
To be consumed in my self-hatred
Is this so different from humanity
Or is this what humanity denies
To be the truth
There is a simple message that is decoded
Within the neurons of our brains
And that is the very reason for living
Striving for purpose
And a want to change the world
Something holds me back
Feeling like I am stuck in the miry clay
And can't find a way out
I strive to succeed
Held back by a presence within
Dark and evil
I fail time and time again
Is there hope for this lost soul, God
Help me please, I yell
Is there such a thing as life for me
Yes, there is!

MEMORIES

Distant yet close yet far away
The library of memories
Filtered good from bad
Beaten down in torment of the bad
Hope is given in what is good
There are many visions
That collide with the present
The past conflicts with the present
Told from visions of what is today
Tormented by the thought
I will lose more in the future
Burdens will fall upon those I love
Because of this I will begin to fade away
Haunted by my death seen in many ways
Running into the wave
Of faces met before seen
Seeing what can happen
Sends fear through the veins
Of a tormented soul
Being eaten alive
By words not spoken

HOPE

There are things in this world
That can't be explained
But the possibilities
Are not limited by the things we know
There are always things
Which can be captured
By the glimpse of an eye
Our eyes are our world
So look for the doors that are open
And shut the ones
Which you do not wish to take
Keeping in mind that there are obstacles
That get in the way
Of your life
Move forward and take a grip
Around the life you want
And don't hold back
Succeed in the way you choose
Persevere
Control the catastrophic bullshit
That brings you down
Damn the shame
And loneliness
And despair
Do not let the things of this world
Bring you down
Do it in moderation
And don't let self-doubt
Be the conqueror of your mind
Renew your mind
By the way you have come to understand
To do it
Stand up for yourself
And do not let this world bring you down
But hold onto those that you love

And show love
To others through kindness
I will display kindness
By being there for a friend
That needs to get to a meeting
Through helping people
When something is bringing them down
Through a simple hello
By giving my money
To help expand a ministry
This is what gives a hope to live
To try to help people
Even though confliction arises
Amongst personalities of all
In a sense
A simple complexion of ourselves lives
Within others
And we see in others what we don't like
About our own self complexion
Which makes it hard sometimes
When we look past it
There are always opportunities
To show love

TOGETHER

Can there be a difference
Between me and everyone else
Or are we all the same
With different personalities
What are the things that make us similar
Are they there to teach us about each other
What becomes of us as a whole race
Do we find the things that keep us together
Do we find the things that pull us apart
We need to come together
In companionship
And learn to live together
What are the things we need to do
To accomplish these simple necessities
Can we live
Without hatred for one another
And without fear of one another
Together in unity
Is the easiest way to live together
Where unity exists is where freedom lies.

THE HARD CHOICE

What am I doing in this desolate land
Why does it feel like I am going through
The vast plains of the wilderness
I stand alone
Yet I feel a presence guiding me
So I am no longer alone
I am among someone higher than oneself
And walking hand in hand
What do I do now from this point
Do I follow my higher power
Or do I go my own way
It is a choice that is hard
To walk and to make
I see things from both perspectives
So I stand on both sides of the fence
Where it is not safe
And I remain in the wilderness
Because of my lack of choice
I am alone again
I need to figure it out
So I need to make a choice

SHAME

Do I just sit on it
Till the guilt
Overtakes me
Shame and disappointment
Overtakes me
Like the blood that flows through me
Beating myself up
I can't put the bat away
Bruised and beaten I hold on
And get back up
And keep on fighting
How do I let go of all this
Why is this pain
So comfortable and cunning
Why do I always return to it
And can't let go
Let it go
I tell myself
Still it lingers within myself
So I grip on to someone
Tell them what is going on
And I stop losing the battle

DOOM & GLOOM

There is a pattern to be decoded
Comprised of different shades of black
Embedded within the souls of humanity
It blooms rancid petals
Pressed down by the grip that fear has on us
Placed in the hearts of damned souls
A blanket of darkness covers us
How do we escape what is coming to us all
How do we let go of what is lost
Is there any peace left amongst us
The lost and the pondered
We are withered down and broken
Caught up in the endless abyss
Trying to push through our inevitable doom
We are placed out of whack
In a world so cold
There is a madness that is so bittersweet
That drives us all to the brink of what is
Powered by a glimpse of lust
Which is death
Insanity grips the soul of man
Captured by the things that will come

LOST

What happens when all is lost
When all goes away
And you don't know
What to do
Where does the time go
When all is lost
And we fade away
Is this God's generosity
Here today
Gone tomorrow
What is it then
That we hold onto
Is it the concept of disbelief
What will change from all this
Will the world stop beneath our feet
When will all this stop eating at me
Will it ever go away
Will I continue
To blow in the wind life chaff
Like I am lost
And there is no hope

AMONGST THE RUBBLE

Is there life amongst the rubble
Does it poke its head out so you can see it
Or does it hide
And look like a blemish upon the bliss
Is there hope amongst the rubble
Does it seem
As if everything is hopeless and in doubt
I watch as things change
Amongst the rubble
The pieces start coming together
In one piece
The picture changes now
There is no rubble anymore
But a complete statue
There is hope now
As things come together
I see the pieces working out their kinks
And hope returns to me
As life changes me
Amongst the rubble.

MY PRISON THE MIND

What is this condemning feeling
Is it brought up upon by a simple mistrust
Is this a completely different story
Brought upon me by a lie
Am I tricking myself to believe it
What is happening to me
Is this just a distorted thought
Roaming through my head
Why do I feel alone
In the library of memories
I stand alone
In my mind
Filtering my memories
Why do I feel stuck within myself
Like a prison
Trapped in a shell
Compiled within the circuits of neurons
My mind lets go
and overtakes me
Looking for more knowledge to digest
To compile
To learn
Of events to come

WISDOM

What are the simple consumptions of life
A little bit of change at a time
A time to change the things you can
And the wisdom to know the difference
Between what you can change
And what you can't change
What are these simple complex situations
Taunting me to change who I am
Why should I change
Who I am
To learn
And to grow
In my life
So I can live my life

FALLEN SOLDIERS

Is this aspiration
As I walk along the gravestones
Is this the only form of peace
That I know
I walk along the gravestones
Along the green grass
Fed by the dead
Is this a conspiracy
That the dead feed the living
Is this the desperation
Of the dead wanting to live on
I continue to walk
As I count the graves
The loss of life is a sad story
The loss of soldiers
That have laid it all on the line
Their stories live on
Battle worn, I am
I send out to my brothers in arms
My respects to them
For what they have accomplished
Through their lives
Their stories are heard
All around the world
The people cry
For their loved ones
I reach the gravestone
Which I was looking for
I say
I love you, Grandpa

SIN

I speak in a silent whisper
I sin out the tongue of man
Bothered by what comes out
I sit in silent sunder
I speak out louder now
And watch the world change
I am watching one day at a time
Watching the sea of faces
Move and flow through the streets
Watch as I capture sin in many ways
Watch closely as the world changes
I hear the voices in my head
The voices of many
Telling me what to do
I hear the sin of man while I listen
To the conversations of many
Life changes right before our eyes
The concept of
See no evil
Hear no evil
Speak no evil
Runs rampant through humanity
A change occurs through all of us
When a simple glimpse of light
Changes everything for all

GRAVITY

What is the intensity
Of this fatality in which I live
Is this the capacity
Which we reach in the mind
A favorable life which brings great wonder
What are the wonders of this world
A compassion for the futility of this life
What is the mass of volume of what is
Is this what weighs us down
The gravitational pull of gravity
The world spins
But we stand still
Move like ants to the ant farm
Pressures of the work placed down upon us
What is all this for
Will this end with a fatality which we await
Is the world pulling us back down
Into the ground from which we came
Into the dark abyss of dirt and green grass
These are the forces of nature
And probabilities to come

IN TIME

Caught up in a simple situation
Can't you even see the truth
Blessed in every way imagined
But beaten down by the things I do
I watch my world fall apart
I see the things that hold me back

I want to see you
But I have a hard time
I see your face within time
Then I watch you fade away
What do I do then
When all I want is you
I will see you again in time

What are these simple expectations
That you expect of me
Will they bring me down again
Will you help me figure it out
I watch my world fall apart
I see the things that hold me back

Broken and bothered
By these realities I see
I'm weakening
And fall by myself
I watch the world fall down
Fall down upon my head

SITTING

Watching the time as time slowly passes
Listening to the secrets of others
Sitting pondering what to do
I sit in silence amongst people
Yet I feel alone
And feel like I am going
Against the grain
Is this part of my insanity
Feeling alone amongst people
I watch and laugh
With great confidence
As we joke amongst each other
What do I do when all is quiet
I sit and listen
And learn a thing or two

ALAN

I miss you so much
You were always there for me
You taught me
How to play the bass
I love you so much for that
You were always there to talk to
When things were going wrong
We would sit for hours
And laugh the days away
You were the best at guitar
I was your #1 fan
You could sit and learn a song
As fast as I could speak
You were always there for me
Till you died of your disease
You hit a van and were smashed
The pain of the steering wheel
Digging into your chest
You killed two people
A pregnant woman and her kid
You will always be a part of me
You will be in my heart
You belong with God now
And I will see you
On the other side

FUCK THIS PLACE

Fuck it all
Fuck this world
Fuck everything you stand for
Don't belong
Don't exist
Don't give a shit
Don't ever judge me
Be who you want to be
Don't let people push you around
Stand up for yourself and fight
Till you get your rights
Tell everyone to fuck off if you have to
Who gives a shit about this world
That is so full of hatred
Why is there so much
I do not know
But hatred is good sometimes
If you like it or not
Without it, all we are is a pussy fuckin planet
So fuck everything in the world
Just let me be who I am
If you don't, fuck you fuckers in the world
Why are people so hypocritical in the world
I don't give a shit
Why can't people be more like me
Fuck you, fuck you mother fuckers
You will all die by my hands, in the end
Boo hoo, I killed your child
I don't give a shit
I will take your head
And stick it on a stake
You like that
This will happen to all, in the end

WONDERLAND

welcome to the
wonderland
where everything is fun
this is the place you want to come
to make your wishes come true
where everyone gets along
you won't ever see a fight
welcome to the place
where evil is gone
everywhere you look
you see giant mushrooms
and bees harvesting LSD
so watch out for their stings
you will never come down again
you will trip for life
when it snows
it is powders of every kind
the trees grow ex
and any other drug
welcome to the place
where everything is free
you see giant worms
smoking from hookas
he will ask you to join
you can see little dwarves
working the fields
the fields of bud
you can see as far
as you can see
welcome to wonderland
which is the place
to live

SLEEPING

this is the way
I would like to die
I don't care how it happens
as long as I am not
awake
you can stab me
over and over
you can stick a pillow
over my face
and suffocate me
or if everything else fails
take a knife
and slit my throat
I most likely wish
it to be from natural causes
I choose this manner to die
because you wouldn't feel
a thing
I would like to die
in peace
and without any pain
this is my wish to die in bed
there is no better way
besides dying from
old age
so please let my life end
in my bed
let me sleep forever
in my death bed
let my body rot
I will lay in my death bed
for all eternity

THE NETHERLANDS
OR HEAVEN

Let me see the gates above
let the doves shit on my grave
let my body decompose
let my soul fly free
put my soul to rest
put me in a better place
I don't want to hear
those bells of Satan
crawling up on me
let the insects eat me
till there is nothing left
or at least let me go
in between heaven and hell
so I can be a spirit
who roams free
I can go place to place
without being seen
I'd rather be with my father
up in the clouds above
I will get a new body
and sing all day
with praise
I wish not to be with Satan
who is as evil as can be
he will set my soul ablaze
and feel pain
for all eternity
this I do not want
so send me to the
Netherlands
or
to the sky's above

BOMBS

the bombs are falling
from the sky
when they hit
everything is set ablaze
you can smell
the smell of death
the smell of flesh
everything is burning
then turns to dust
the bombs
come from the bombers
the bombers above
when they release them
they fall swiftly through the air
when they hit
they detonate
killing everything in sight
bombs are a danger
to everyone in the world
they are used for war
or terrorists
or to juts blow things up
so if you hear one
dropping down on you
don't just stand there
get out of the way
you might not make it
and die anyway

so get down on your knees and pray
so now the bombs are falling
falling from the sky
it's either run and hide
or you will surely die
you will feel your flesh melting
melting from your bones
you might die slowly
from all the radiation
so watch for the bombs
falling from the sky

THE HIGH WAY

today is the day I go insane
while I release drugs into my brain
when I do this I go crazy
when I come down I get lazy
all the craziness in between
is best to use on Halloween
I am the man that flies up high
I don't care about how I die
my eyes are all red and dry
when I think about it I start to cry
it feels like my lungs are going to blow
this is all I have to show
I work my ass off to feed my addiction
now I don't even have a dime to give
for I am an addict living on the streets
for I have nothing to eat
I live my life in poverty
in this fucked up community
I walk around looking dead
while I look for some way to get ahead
I wish I could have straightened my life
I couldn't so I grabbed a knife
I slit my wrist to release the pain
but I was still fucked up and insane
I stuck a needle in my spine
I felt the drugs stream through my veins
I fell to the ground because I blacked out
I awake with a shout
as I sit there in my blood

I began to realize this is not the life for me
but it was too late for me
I lost to much blood to live
I am getting cold
then I lay there till there was nothing
I am dead now
can't you see
this was the way
my life
is to be

THE PASSION I LOVED

I had a passion
I gave it up
So I can live my life
The right way
I love this passion so much
I did what I could
To do it
I would steal
To do it
This passion I loved so much
I did it because
I was addicted to this passion
This passion
Brought me down in the end
It caused me to almost die
That is when I got scared
Then, in the end, my passion
Took my step-dad
Who had the same passion as me
To go out and get fucked up
And to live my life this way
Then I put myself into treatment
So I could leave
This passion I loved
All I have to say is
I will miss you
And good-bye, in the end

LOVE FOR DRUGS

I was sitting in my room
The room was spinning
I couldn't sleep
I was scared
I was seeing things I should have not
It was all in my head
It was all the drugs in my system
It was all going to my spine
I knew what I did was a crime
I didn't care
I needed to get fucked up
I did every drug that came my way
I didn't have anything to say
I kept on using
I was numb
From my toes to my legs
I did too much
I am drooling
I went to my room again
And passed out
I began to OD
On acid
And many other
Drugs
I did not survive
Because of my love for drugs

PARANOID

where ever I go
I feel people are
watching me
watching my every move
I wish I could walk somewhere
and not feel this way
for I am paranoid
from all the drugs I have done
for I am scared inside
because I see shadows
following me
following me through the dark
for I am paranoid
and I think everyone is after me
this is scary to me
seeing things that aren't there
I wish these visions and feelings
would go away
because they are driving me insane
for I am paranoid
of everything
and everyone
even till this day

MY LIFE ON DRUGS

I love the way you make me feel
you make me feel so real
I love you in my life
and it is so hard to say good-bye
I love the way I fly up high
thinking I can never die
I will say bye someday
but I don't know when
I know I can't do it by myself
but that is all I have
all I have to say
this isn't working out
but that is so hard to believe
when I keep on turning back
I struggle with sobriety
because you are in my life
I tried so hard to stay away
but you are always there
you were my whole world
and I want to say good-bye
while sometimes you make me want to die
but I go back to hide my true feelings
then I take a look and realize I am dying
I want to say good-bye
but this is so hard
because you will always torment me
when you want to feed on me
you gradually kill me

I must find a way to escape
but this is hard because you are how I escape
so I go out and go insane
for you are the one to blame
and you are the one that eats my brain
and eats away my organs
but this is my disease
maybe this is the way I will die
but I don't know
but this life on drugs
and I am stuck with it
till the end

THIS LOVE

There is a girl I love so much
She makes me feel so loved
I want to be with her someday
For this I will pray
I like the way
We understand one another
When I go and talk to her
I begin to stutter
Then she begins to smile
A smile I love so much
Then she looks me in the eye
And says everything will be ok
I love those blue eyes she has
They put me in a daze
When she turns around
Her hair flies through the air
When I look into the emptiness
Of her long black hair
I wish I could tell her how I feel
I don't know what to say
I can say one thing
I am in love

DON'T FUCK WITH ME

Don't fuck with me
I will bring you down with me
I got shit on you
that you think no one knows
I will do things I don't want to
To find out this shit
So don't fuck me over
If you do
You will go to jail
I will be laughing at you
You will be crying
For what you did to me
In the end, everything goes as planned
So fuck you damn hoe
So next time you fuck with me
Make sure you find out shit
Because if you go down
Next time you will bring me with you
And if you don't
I will send you off
On another journey
When will you learn
Not to fuck with me
You know what will happen
So next time you fuck with me
Make sure you have shit on me
I can get you with petty shit
You have to get something big
So have fun crying
As you sit in jail

GENOCIDE

Why kill off a race
They did nothing to you
They are either shot
Or burn you
For nothing you did
Why kill off a race
You know this is wrong
Why do you have problems
With this race
Why do you kill them
Shoot them down
In big groups of people
Or stick them in an oven
And let them burn
You are nothing but
Racist mother fuckers
Why do you have to kill
An entire race
To get your point across to people
That you don't like them
This is scary
Think if you were in that situation
Where you were going to be killed
For nothing
Because of your race
Kill everyone
That is of this race
Till there is none
None of them
Left in the world

24 HOURS

Some days go bad
Some days go good
The good days go fast
The bad days go slow
Don't think about tomorrow
Don't think about yesterday
Otherwise you are pissing on today
Every day is a struggle
If you live this kind of life
Some days you are at war
Some days you are not
If you are just pick up the phone
Every day you have to be honest
Honest with yourself
And other people
Do this everyday
And you will be fine
Go to a meeting
Pick up the phone
Do this everyday
If you have the time
Do it for yourself
And no one else
Do this everyday
For 24 hours

ON THE RUN

I am running away
Running away from everyone
And everything
I don't know where to run
I have nowhere to go
And if I turn back
I will be sent to jail
Because I know my mom
Has called the cops by now
The cops are after me
This is all I do now
Run like hell
To keep from going to jail
I sleep in the dumpsters
I have been raped up the ass
What else could happen
I could be killed
Or be beaten to the ground
Life on the streets is not fun
When you have no place to go
Everyone thinks I am dead now
I heard it on the news
I have been gone for months now
And all I do is scrounge up money
Money to eat, money to live
So I don't die on the streets
and become a fossil
I have decided to go home now
And live my life the right way
Go home and sleep in a bed
Which I haven't done for months
For I have slept on the streets
this is not the life for me

ATTRACTED

I am attracted to people
I need them to live my life
Without friends in my life
I am nothing but alone
So I attract myself to people
So I don't feel alone
Sometimes this attraction
Leads me to getting stoned
It also leads to sober friends
Who got my back in the end
These are the friends
I am attracted to now
Because they make my life better
They bitch
When things are going wrong for me
This is better now than never
For this attraction to sober friends
Is better off than dead
I hope this attraction
For these people
Stays with me till the end

THE ADDICT

What the fuck is up
I am
I feel all the drugs
Flowing through my veins
I am numb as can be
This is the way I will stay
It scares me sometimes
It brings me down
It makes me go insane
You don't want to know
What is going through my brain
It drives me crazy
So I smoke some more
One is not enough
So I do a lot more
I would turn on my friends
To go find more drugs
Because they did not have any
And I needed some more
I lost many friends
Because I was dumb
People called me names
Names that hurt
I was just living life my way
Not the way you wanted
So let me use
Let me fly free
Fuck you all and just let me be
I am alone
I am scared
Because no one loves me
Because I am an addict

A SHOUT FOR HELP

Why do people cut
To get rid of emotional pain
There are so many different ways
To get rid of the pain
I have never cut myself
Bleeding on the floor
You can get help for that
If you really want it
Don't waste your life away
What is the point
Of cutting your wrist
Why don't you hang yourself
And get it over with
If you want to kill yourself
And do it the right way
I know all you are looking for
Is a way out of life
Or
You are giving a shout for help
I will only help
If you are giving a shout for help
If not
You can die in the end
I am not saying I don't care
I will give you support
If you really want it
I will help you out
When you are not alright up there
I will always be there
To help you in the end

OBSESSED

I love the way you make me feel
all I have to say is I love you
you make me feel all good inside
if you were gone I would like to die
I love your smile
and your nice red lips
they remind me of roses
All I want is to be with you
because you make my life complete
you are part of my soul
all I did was show you love
I am hated by you now
you broke my heart in two
and smashed it on the ground
thinking you would never let me go
I never thought you would do this to me
why did it come down to this
I am scared without you
but this is the way it has to be
I miss my love
I miss you lots
but in the end
shy did this happen to me
I miss seeing you everyday
your smile that made me shine
I will never forget you
I will get you back
I will do what I have to
even if it means to kill
because I want you so bad
and I will get you in the end

PEDOPHILE

You are sick in the head
And twisted in the head
I wish I could leave you for dead
For when you touched me
I was scared
You did it without a care
You said you would beat me if I told
Then you began to grip a hold
You began to molest me
This is fucked up, you see
How could you do this to me
Touch me where you want
This is my life forever
This memory will never leave
When I began to think about it
I began to cry
I get depressed about it
Wishing I could die
So why did you shove
Your finger in my ass
It hurt to sit down in the grass
When you sucked my dick
It made me feel sick
When you tried to kiss me
I didn't want to see
I laughed when you went to jail
Without any bail
I hope you got killed there
That way, it would be fair
Because you aren't nothing special
but a pedophile

FALLEN

I am frying
I am dying
I am falling from the sky
Down beneath
Where there is nothing
But pain
I am falling
But I can't get up
I am held down
To the ground
By a force that won't
Let loose
I try to escape
This world of emptiness
No matter how hard I try
I can't succeed
What can I do so that
I can succeed
I don't know
My mind is confused
It is wrapped full of secrets
I can't let go
This drags me down
I have hit rock bottom
I don't care
Everything is hazy
I am going crazy

I lay there on the ground
Looking into space
I feel like I am falling
For all eternity
I cannot land on my feet
I can't bring my self
To get back up
So I fly
Fly away
From everything
Everything in life
And everything
That is me

CUTTING DEEP

I watch
As it forms a stream
A stream of blood
I watch
As it flow down my arm
To the tips of my fingers
I watch
As it drips to the ground
I feel like my life is fading
The blood keeps on flowing
I cannot stop it
Even if I wanted to
I cut too deep
I cut the veins in half
I am scared
I have emotions
Running through my head
I know pretty soon
That my life will end
I don't wish to live
This life
This life of pain
And suffering
So I take the blade
And cut in deep
So I can't stop the bleeding
I sit in the tub

With blood streaming from my veins
Everything is getting cold
You know what is happening
I am about gone
My soul
Will leave my body
I can't feel now
For my body is numb
This is the end now
I will see you
In the next life
Life after death

MY ACTIONS

My actions
Are my decision
There is nothing you can do
To change this
What I think
Is what goes
You cannot make me change
I know I am stubborn
But this is the way it is
I hate actions sometimes
Because they get to places
I don't want to go
And sometimes they get me
To go out and get stoned
If I don't straighten up
I will live on the streets
Because of my decisions
This is the way it must be
Right now, I am at war with my mind
Over a disease
Because of this it brings me down
Making me go use
But I don't
And my decision is made
This' been going on
For a couple days now
It is driving me insane

I am going crazy
Over the decisions I have made
My actions are good now
For this is my decision
I lay in bed
And twitch all night
Wishing I could use
But it is just a thought
That I don't go through with
Because this is the action
I decided on
And this is the way it will stay

CONGRATULATIONS

Keep up the good work you have done
90 days is better than none
Don't look backward
Don't look forward
Look at today and not tomorrow
Otherwise you will feel sorrow
You worked so hard for your sobriety
It's so hard out in the community
I will be there if you need support
It is way better than going back to court
You have worked so hard to get there
I thank you for stopping to share
I am so proud of you
I hope you choose the right thing to do
Take a look at me, right now
And tell me what you see
All I do is ask for help
And that is what I receive
You helping me
Is inspiring me to recover
You are on a roll now
Your life is getting better
Don't give up on yourself
When things go bad
Just think back
To when you were going mad
All I have to say
Congratulations on your 90 days

POSSESSED

I am sick of running
From all this sin
All this sin
Running through my veins
I feel evil calling me
Calling me with the numbers

666

My soul is gone
I gave it
To the devil
He is in me
I can feel it
He took control
Of my soul and body
You look into my eyes
And see blood and fire
These are some things
That he desires
Death, hatred, and lust
Are things that I was given
He took me over with a touch
A touch of pain and suffering
He looked inside my body
And saw the things he loved
He brought my soul
To the gates of hell
And my body was left above
Satan did this to me
And left me above
Left me above
Possessed
With his soul

ILLUSIONS

I am on a killing spree
I am a murdering fiend
I am out to kill
I have the thirst for blood
while I stab the stupid broad
I felt my strength
in killing you
what am I to do
I just kill for fun
even your little son
it is all exciting to me
while I began to stitch
I cut the victim open
then I take his kidneys
then I take a thread
and sew into his head
I sewed his mouth and eyes shut
so he wouldn't yell
or even take a peek
I then took his nuts
and began to cut them off
then I left him there for dead
while he bled to death
I didn't give a fuck
because it was all fun and games
now that I think about it

I was insane
because I took some acid
it made me see these things
now that I know what was wrong
it was all in my head
I was tripping on acid
I saw the kid was dead
I was just having a bad trip
it was all just image
going through my head
when I came down
no one was dead

GOOD-BYE

I am flying up high
high into the sky
wishing this dream
would not go away
I see the drugs
from every direction
they won't stop coming
what am I going to do
I am dumb
feeling numb
bring me back to my reality
This is normal
I am not scared now
I don't feel pain
I am going insane
I can gradually feel
life leaving me
I just stare into the air
with a blank stare
with nothing to fear
I steer my life in the wrong direction
I can't help it
I just feed into my disease
I sit in the same room
with the same people
wish I could die up high
I sit and smoke an ounce
as if it were nothing
I don't care if it
eats my body
as long as I get high
but in the end

I went to treatment to straighten
out my life
I hated it
I was not the same
that place drove me insane
when I got out
I stayed clean for a couple weeks
I went on a binge
I wasn't going to stop
then I got the support from
from friends and family
then I said good-bye
to my disease

FRIENDS WITH TRUST

I am sick of all the mistrust in my life
There are many I can trust
The people I trust are
Always there for me
They are always there to
Support me
They give me good advice
When things are going wrong
They make me feel so strong
All the ones I thought I trusted
They left me for drugs
The ones that didn't
They stuck it out till I left
Those are the ones I love
Those are the ones
I trust
The ones who don't leave me
For drugs
Those are the ones I live
To trust
Because they have my back

FIGHTING WITH COURAGE

I am a soldier
I go down fighting
Fighting for a country
That means nothing to me
I fight with courage
Against the enemy
I fight with courage
To see if I go home
Because if I don't
I go to prison for treason
So I fight the war with courage
I might die
I might live
But I won't find out
Till the end
I am scared
I shoot to live
I do this with strength
And hope
But in the end
I want to go home
So I fight this war
With courage

OUTCAST

How different are we
From everyone else
Not at all
We are normal people
With a normal gift
We are not to be pushed away
Like outcasts
What do we do
To let our support know
We are alright
Do we sit back
And just let things happen
Do we have the time
To fix the problems that taunt us
Should I move on
And be more open
About my illness in my mind
There are times
Where I repress it all
In fear of the alternative
Is there anyone I can trust
Why don't people understand
I am not crazy
I am a normal human being
And the same person

ANGER

What is anger
The emotion that
Stuffs all other emotions
What do you do with your anger
Do you stuff it inside
Till you explode
Or do you express
And bring healing to the situations
What triggers your anger
Is it the mix of emotion
Being held within your very being
Why do we stuff our anger
Is it a fear
Of losing control
Is it a fear
Of rejection
What we need to know
Is that anger comes out regardless
Does anger impair your relationships
Yes
You take your anger out
On other people
What comes out the mouth
Is from the heart
There are reasons
For stuffing anger
So that you
Can avoid confrontation
And let a situation slide
The whole point
Is not to get stuck
In your anger

CHANGE

Where did life go
Did it blow away
Like chafe in the wind
Did it go
Where the wavering wave goes
What happens
When the wind blows
And dandelions blow away
Spreading its seed
Always growing
Is this what life is
Changes and opportunities
Waiting to grow
Watch closely
And watch the world change
Right before your eyes
Is this a glimpse
Of reality that we live with
Seeing the simplicity
Of a situation
That we have no control
What do we do then
Do we sit around
Waiting for life's situations
To overtake us
Do we try to change
What we can
And let life change from there

Life is an ongoing commitment
To change
And pursuit of happiness
A calamity
Which is an ongoing struggle
For humanity
Humanity struggles
One day at a time
What is this circle we live in
And do we change this process
The process to do things differently
So that people have an opportunity
To do something different
What do we do from here
Live life on life's terms
With an opportunity to see things
You have never seen before
Through the eyes
Of a changed man

PAIN

Is there 1,000 things humanity can't fathom
And these things brought to us
Which are seldom
Is this a circle which we can't escape
Are we like Superman without his cape
Are these the realities
To which we come to believe
Are these the lies within us
Which bring relief
Are we caught up
Within the belly of the beast
Being beaten within
Like a monster that wants release
Tamed by the temptation
Which we are given in
Inside is the urge to give in, into sin
Does peace come
When the battle rages
Or does it just keep coming
For all the ages
Is this the battle we face
For all eternity
Or will I end up
Back in the infirmary
The darkest things within my heart
Hold me down
Sometimes it is like this makes me feel
Like I have drowned
Is there nothing
That can bring back to the light
Not if you are not willing to fight

Is there anything worth fighting for
Or do we just pick the scab off the sore
What is this continual cycle
Of pain and suffering
Does it ever go away
Or is this just a time of buffering
Compiled in the smut of this world
What do you do
Sit in the muddle in your past
Do you dwindle upon the future
What is lost
You give into bliss and pain
This where it must end

LIFE & DEATH

This is the way things come together
Through the revelation of life and death
Brought forth by the struggle
In which we live
Where there is life
There is love
And where there is death
There is fear
Love and fear
Is what makes up life and death
There is a great perspective between the two
Life brings freedom
And hope and love
Death brings hatred,
Malice and failure
I see these things
And it brings peace to me
Yet is also brings
Poverty and despair
This is the concept
We all need to deal with
That we all fall into the concept
Of life and death
And we must choose it
One day at a time

FALLING DEEP

Falling deep
To the emptiness
Of my dark mind
I can't see in light
Only in dark of night
My thoughts are frightening
But are relaxing
My thoughts are not for people
But they are always there
I can't hear you
But someone else
I see things
That you can't see
I won't let anyone know
What I hear or see
But all I do
Is fall deep
Into the pit
In the back
Of my dark mind

THE JOURNEY

Is this a story
Which was foretold for centuries
A journey to take place
Amongst the realms
Is this a journey
To the catacombs
To define life as I know it
Is it good or bad
To take these steps
Take these steps
To put that 9 to my head
And pull the trigger
This is the beginning
Of the dream
The journey
Of complicated suicide
And to get
The keys of hell
Here I am
Committing every sin in the book
To achieve my goal
Every time I die
Something bigger happens
To this world
More people die
With no remorse
Change overtakes me
And I begin not to care
Death after Death
I become hardened to the bone
I achieve my goals
And come out
Of the bottomless pit
I kill two prophets
And gain two more keys

I begin to chase a woman
But she is protected by God
So I wait
And bring destruction upon this world
I then devour the woman
After the birth of the child
And I am defeated
I get the last key
I am in heaven now
Where I play music
And am a top angel
In God's Army
Then I use God's knowledge
To betray him
A great battle waged
And I was thrown out of heaven
Into hell
Where I fought for my throne
I bound Satan
And took my spot
In the underworld
This is my journey
The journey in my dream.

BURIED ALIVE

I can feel insects inside
Eating me as I start to die
Trapped in a box
I can't move
I can't breathe
I am suffocating
I put my hands
To my throat
I begin to struggle
My body goes limp
Now I am gone
The worms dig
Deep into my flesh
And start to eat
My brains
The termites eat
My dead flesh
Which will fall off my bones
Whatever is left
Will soon decay
How would you like
To be buried alive

THE DISABLED

Are we the people you call disabled
Are we your average person
That admits they have a fault
Beaten down
And provoked
By the system telling us
That we are alright
We are people with faults and gifts
That make us very creative
We are the brave souls
Which compel to make change
Within our lives
To better oneself
We are everywhere
And all around
Every one
Willing to help people to understand
What we go through
Isn't everyone in a sense
A little disabled
And filled with mental illness
The only way the world can be so crazy
Is if this is so
Mental illness can go both ways
It can be bad
As well as good

PANIC

Hands on the wheel
Steering down the path of life
On the way to open mic
The land of poetry
What is this feeling
That is overtaking me
Is this the misuse of my meds
That is taking control
Fear fills me up
From the inside out
I go astray from the path
Which I was going on
Is this anxiety taking control
Can I drive my own bus
Can I be myself again
Will this pressure on my chest
Keep me standing still
Unable to move
I pull over
And stop
In an attempt to regain
Control of myself
I do breathing exercises
In, out
In, out
I regain control of myself
I come back to myself
And move on

Still feeling a little panicky
I attempt to drive home
Still feel the anxiety
From the previous attack
On my life
I am able to press forth
I drop a friend off
I made it this far, I tell myself
I drive again
This is the last stretch
Will I make it
Yes, I will tell myself
Anxiety lessens
And I make it home
Where I relax
And win the battle
That overtook me

THE BATTLE

I lie dormant
Within myself
Taken in by the memories
That lay in the distant past
What does the future hold for me
Compiled in thought
The memories taunt me
What lies lay
Within one's heart
Is there a glimpse of hope
That lays within the human soul
The soul is a flame
That brings and gives life
To you
As a person
Light the flame
And hope and life is given freely

Out of the mouth
The heart speaks off the tongue
Fire darts can slip out
Within the soul
Be yourself
And love shall come out your lips
Locking away the beast
The beast will take away your life
If not tamed
And beaten back

Guard what you hear
For what you hear
Is a trickle to the mind
Which gives way
To negativity to the heart
The battle continues
What you see
Is the gateway to the soul
What you see
Can send you into
A traumatizing mental spiral
And bring evil
Into your heart

Is this what life is
A constant battle
Between God
The beast
and yourself

The very aspects of life
Are based off of
See no evil,
Speak no evil,
And hear no evil

SNIPER

I lay in silence in the snow
Quiet and motionless
So no one can see me
I put snow in my mouth
So no one can see my breath
I begin to inch forward
To get into position
I look down my scope
Looking for the enemy
I see my target and I breathe
In, out, my heart racing
I hold my breath as
I lock onto my target
I put my finger on the trigger
And squeeze the trigger
I watch as my target falls
The whole camp goes crazy
I relocate and try again
Two more targets down
I hit the assigned targets
I inch away as
People are chasing me
I run and run
Dogs on the trail
I hide in the brush
Camouflaged in
After misleading the trail
The enemy surround me
But I am not seen by anyone
I creep away
Inch by inch
I escape capture
I make it back to base

EMOTIONS

What emotion would you like to change
Is it the emotions that hold you back
Or strengthen the ones
You want to better yourself with
Is emotion the one thing
That builds your world
Or is it the thing
That tears your life apart
We live a life of emotion
How do you regulate what you feel.
You have to find a way
To control yourself
And how to distract yourself
What can you change
About yourself
When your emotions take over
Does your life go into a downwards spiral
Or do you try to deal with the cards
Which you were dealt
And react in a positive manner
To react with the right reaction
This is the way
You should react
In a manner that is perspective to others

THE WORLD

What happens when you see the world
Through a peek hole
Do we just see a glimpse
Of what this world really holds for us
Does this reality hold true to it's meaning
Is this world just tattered
And torn apart by the seams
Trying to tell us
That there is going to be
A turn of events
That are coming
What do we do
When the world is in shambles
Do we just let it get
Worse and worse
Do we come together
In a chance to change this world
Here we are asking
The same questions
Over and over again
The world turns
And we destroy it
What do we do from here
Come together and fix
What we have destroyed
Will this bring peace
Back to the world
Will we just long for it
And do nothing
To fix this transparency
The world is a beautiful place
And we call it home

(MENTAL)

What is this mental situation
Which occurs within myself
Is it a puzzle we have to keep on
Putting back together again
Is it a dream and
Will I wake up feeling better
I want to see
What happens from this point on
I want to see
A piece of the puzzle added on
So I can accomplish
And grow, mentally
What happens
When the puzzle weakens
I feel, mentally, that I am shutting down
And depression hits me like a brick wall
So I pick up the pieces
And I put them all back together again
For some peace of mind
I have no time for an eventual relapse
I must grip on to reality
And not watch myself fall apart
Is this just part of life
Getting up and falling down
Is this the mental growth process
I want to have a mental award
Where I do not have to worry
About the simple things of life
That the pieces would stay together
And no problems exist

MINDFULNESS

Is the awareness with no limits
And without judgement
You need to take life
On it's own terms
You must accept yourself
As you are
Plus accept people
As they are
In order to have complete mindfulness
We need to look
At the here and now
Not the past
Or the future
At this point
You will be awakened
To life on its terms
With practice
You can do this
By directing your attention
To one thing
In the moment
Mindfulness allows you to observe
Life's situations
Through description
And participation
Don't evaluate and
Unglue your opinion
And accept each moment
Acknowledge help
And don't judge your judging
There are ways
To be mindful

Do one thing at a time
Let go of the things
That hold you back
And distract you
And concentrate your mind
Stay alert to your thoughts
Watch your thoughts
Coming and going
Be cautious
of what comes through your senses
So become one with your experience
Completely forgetting yourself
So Act
Intuitively
From wise mind
So Practice.

DEPRESSION

What happens
When anger is not dealt with
Does numbness flow through you
Into a deep depression
Do you know what you feel
Half of the time
In the deep abyss
What emotion should I feel
When I am like this
Every emotion
Is better than this
The emotion does not stay
All the time
No matter how long it may last
The way it affects you may change
Isolation is not an alternative
To depression
To have people around
Helps keep us up and active
And lessens the effects
The depression has on us
Depression does not make us
Who we are
But it can stop us in our tracks
So do not feel hopeless
When your emotions catch up to you
But stand strong
And let your life be lived out
And let peace fill you
There is a time to fall
But there is always
A time to stand back up

CHURCH

People come and gather
In a time of fellowship
Brought there
Guided
By the presence of God
We come together
In love and amity
Which brings us into unity
With God and other people
Hope for more
For the world in God's plan
It is a place of safety
For lost souls and
For those that are not
A place to bring
Serenity and peace
To the spirit
In which God bears witness
It is a time to learn
And a time to grow
It is a place where we go
To let God turn over our will
And put our lives into God's care
We go to praise and worship
God as we understand Him
We go to learn
About
Faith, hope, and love
The greatest of these
Is Love

(MIND)

Is there peace of mind
Within the human soul
Do our minds just race
Nonstop
Consuming
Our inner spirit
Does our heart
Sometimes deceive us
Into doing things
We don't want to
What brings us together
The electrical neurons
Within our brain
Tying us together
Is this the power of our minds
That there are things
That happen inward
That appear outward
Does our mind work
Off the things we see
And the things we hear
And that's it
No
It works more on a subconscious level

Telling us what to do
What to do
If our minds control us
On another level
From emotional, physical, mental
Do we have any control
Or are we insane
And have no control
Over our lives
Mentally, we lose control
And learn
With what comes our way
This is our mind

SUICIDAL TENDENCIES

I feel as if no one cares
Cares about me
Or how I feel
This is sad to me
Because I care
But depression hits me
With a stare
It stares me in the eye
And beats me down
To me this isn't fair
I cut my wrist
To release the pain
Otherwise it will drive me insane
I am scared to let people know
Know how I feel
It hits me hard
In the heart
And makes me ill inside
But I am still here today
Sticking it out
But all I want
Is to lash out
And shout
I want to tell how I feel
I don't know how to say it
So I stuff it deep inside
And inside it will stay
Someday I wish I could die
And fly up into the sky
But I don't
Because I belong
On this world

I stay because of the people I will hurt
And I don't want
To watch them cry
Over my grave
So I take all
Take all this pain
And hold it deep inside
I almost killed myself
Too many times
That is not the way to go
So I stopped with the guilt trip
And now I have friends today
I live my life
As a normal kid now
This is the life for me
So in the end
This is the way
I am going to be

PEACE OUT

why can't you see
what is happening to me
take a look inside
and it will make you cry
I grew up wanting to die
I have failed everything I try
what is the point of living
when no one gives a fuck
I don't like myself
any more than you do
I am a failure
why do you make me feel
so immature
as I look down
there is a sea of blood
I don't care
for I am not loved
I am hated by everyone
in the end
I will go down below
in the end
why does everyone tease me
I don't know
why did everyone beat me
into the dirt
I am alone now
laying in my tub
the water I lay in
is as red as can be
as I lay there waiting to die
I sit there and cry
for the worthless life I live

I sit
and watch the blood drip
from my wrist
as everything is hazy
from the lack of blood
I sit there
I cannot see
for I am dead now
see you later
peace out

THINGS UNKNOWN

There are lots of things
Unknown to the world
Why does the government
Hide so much from us
I am scared of the things
That are hidden
There are so many hidden wars
Wars of hunger
National resources
And land
Why don't they tell us
Of Genocide
If they would tell us
We could help
Help the world
And its people
There are so many things
That the government keeps hidden
What else is out there
We don't know
There are so many things
Not discovered
Like diseases
Medicines
And technology
There is a list of unknown things in the world
But the things that are known
Are kept a secret
There are also weapons and alien artifacts
That are hidden from us all
This is why I hate the government
Because they hide so much
and keep things unknown

SOFTENING THROUGH LOVE

I write to preserve
What is honest
Not giving up
Written
Not giving up
On hope
Becoming what is new
Renew what is me
I change into a new form
Of what is me
Changing into a life
That is full of purpose
Living a day at a time
I press forward
Overcoming
And persevering
Through the trials of life
I hold onto life
Always changing
Always pressed
I see a new life
I see clearly
And move forward
With a softened heart
I then become
What is me
A person with purpose
And held together
Through love

OVERCOMING THE TRIALS

I live a new day
Not giving up on life
I fail to renew my thoughts
But I keep on moving on
I love the fact
That every time I fail
I grow and learn
And turn into a new me
Learning and becoming
A person of interest
I hate that
Every day seems familiar
But I love the fact
That I learn something
Everyday
About myself
Growing and blossoming
Into the perfect me
Perfect in Spirit
Imperfect in the physical
But always changing
I seek more than I previously knew
I want more
What is the truth
I don't know
Cause I am stuck
Between mental illness and reality
I still grip to reality
And overcome
The trials of life

THANK GOD

I breathe
Hoping to see a glimpse
Of forgiveness
I know what I have done
Beaten down
By my own thoughts
I need to forgive myself
Otherwise
I will remain the drunk I am
I want more
Than I have right now
A new life
Full of purpose
I need more
I want more
I want to see
Where God takes me from here
I believe it will be
Complete
In the way He planned
My life to be
Always foretold
Before I was born
He leads me upon
The road of life
I love You
And thank You

A LIFE WORTH LIVING

I believe in hope
Without hope
There is no life worth living
There has to be more
A belief more than one's self
I need to believe in myself
Is this a conspiracy
Or is there a chance to live
Life on life's terms
Is this a tempered knife
Stabbed into my heart
For sometimes
I feel like giving up
But for some reason
I hold on
To the things that matter
I am a schizo
Caught up in my thoughts
I am sorry to be so negative
But I struggle with my mind
Which drives me crazy
But I try to think
Of the good things
Not the bad
Sometimes I can't think
About how much life sucks
Getting through the tough times
Builds strength
Helping you grow
I believe in myself
And live to serve
With much belief
A life worth living

DAY AT A TIME

A breath
A glimpse in a day
The separation of
Night and day
A simple thing
As breathing can be
The difference
Between life and death
There is a purpose for both
I see crimson when life is lost
I see light when life is given
Which brings a new day
There is only one day
At a time
For you never know
Where death creeps up on you
Taking away the life
That you know
After death
Is the resurrection of the soul
A new life begins
All is taken away
Or is restored
And reborn
And a new life begins
For all life is given
One day at a time
Is there a future
I know there is a past
So I keep on breathing
One day at a time

GIVE PRAISE

(I FAIL TO GIVE GOD EVERYTHING)

I see myself kneeling down
Before my Lord
I pray for the forgiveness
Of my sin
I put Him above all
And thank Him
For every day I have
I want to press forward
And think heavenly
I struggle to do so
I say I am sorry, Lord
For falling short of Your glory
I see You and
You are always on my heart
I need You
I want You
I will always press forward
With You
I don't know what I will do
Without You
I just keep pushing
I know I struggle
To get to know You
I need to learn
To seek You
Become more like You
I need more of You

Of all things
I need to learn
To follow You
I believe in You
I want to become
More like You
Like You said
The greatest form of love
Is to lay down your life
For your friend
I admit that I fail to do so
I do believe in You
And I love everything
You do for me

LOVE NOT DEATH

I watch
As we kill each other
There is always a glimpse
Of life and death
A blink
A bother
A simple lapse
Of what is
I see my breath
A breach in my lungs
Showing that my life is real
Not a false reality
The breath of my life
Shows that I am alive and well
A belief that my soul is intact
I reach out to touch
The hearts of others
Bring life to those around me
A simple gesture
A simple hello
Brings hope to the life
Of those in poverty
I want to see change in my life
But why do I always find myself
On the path of death

A life of sin
There is always the realization
That there is life after death
Always a time to change
The path which I am on
I seek eternal life
Not the life of gnashing of teeth
A brush of death
A glimpse of hell
Burned into my brain
So I breathe in search of life
Not drowning in my regret
Living in my life or hell
I try to live in love
Not death

MY DARKEST HOUR

I am the darkest of all matters
Is this my blessing or is it my curse
Is it as simple as dying
To reverse this
I hope it is not so
For I feel the pits
Of my hell
A leader
A torturer
And a follower by demons
I sense my demise
And feel like I am rebuked
From heaven
Is this what life is
Do I need to worry about myself
Do I crave the desire
To do that which is heavenly
I do
But I feel condemned
Left behind
So I do the opposite of what I want
I am unworthy
Where is my grace
And mercy
I long for it
I know it is there
Somewhere
In the question
But I feel damned
Beaten down
By my own thoughts and feelings
For I am the damned
And the unfortunate

OUR NEW WORLD

I try to see the stars
The glimmering city lights
Block the view of them
My breath leaves
As I see the planets that exist
A new galaxy exposing itself
Showing a new way of our existence
Are we alone
Or is there something greater
In our universe
What do we know
That exists in this vortex
Of volume and matter
We are still trying to figure it out
I believe there is
A breath of life beyond our planet
I wish to see
What is out there
A new life
A communication between new life
A new being
Is this our new existence
To build on new planets
Trying to not take the world
But the universe
For this is our future
To become more than we ever know

SIMPLE OR COMPLICATIONS

Is life simple
Or is it complicated
I believe it is both
It depends
On the thought processes
Can you put the pieces together
To gather the pieces
To bring life to its fullest
Can life shit in your face
And bring problems
And complications
It can
And can change things
For worse or better
I hope it is for the better
I see things
In a better form of life
A belief in something
That pulls me to the brink
Of what is complicated
Or what life can bring
Everything is supernatural
A spiritual thing
For there is an enemy
Trying to bring us down

Satan
The epitome of false life
The devourer of life
The torturer of souls
Can't have me
There is a belief
That I am forgiven
For things not spoken
But happened
Tearing apart my heart
I begin to change
Into a new person

WANTING / THE WILLING TO PUSH

I remember a time
Of sobriety
For this time
Was the best years of my life
A time of peace
And serenity
Why in my conscious mind
Would I choose to give up
A life of purpose
For something
That is taking my life away
I need repentance
To turn away and
Put back into my life
A breach
Of my soul and heart
A change
A belief
And a renewing of my mind
For my mind
I know can transform my world
Bring back the peace
And serenity
That I once felt
Becoming that person
That people love and appreciate

I miss it
I need it
For it is a hard, long road ahead
Trying to overcome
The obstacles
I have failed to accomplish
In the past
I keep on breathing
Trying to accomplish everything
Through the race
Of life

HAPPY BIRTHDAY

There is a new day
For tomorrow is your birthday
I miss you
I hope to see you soon
There is always a great time
To celebrate the birth of my brother
To congratulate you
On your accomplishments
For surviving the hard times
And becoming a stronger person
You're a survivor
And you keep on pressing on
A man whose life
Is work and love
And lives with purpose
For I love you
And wish you
A happy birthday

THE VISION

I see a raven
Gouging out my eyes
My blood drips onto bloody hands
Forming an image
Of two forms of myself
In one hand
Is an image of myself
Seen through a burning flame
A picture of my soul
Like a burning bush
I ignite for God
In the other hand
I see a figure of myself
With a noose around my neck
The thought
To die to self
To serve God
The two combined
Bringing me closer to God
A want
A need
A belief in something
This is my vision
To draw closer to Him
To follow and become more like Him
So I let the raven take my sight
To bring me to the brink
Of my lost soul
To make me weak
So I depend upon You
So let the raven eat
To make me breathe only for you, Jesus

SUFFERING AND LOVE

I am breathing still
Surprised
But still breathing
For a brush with death
Will make you want life more
Bringing you the realization
Of how important life is
There have been times
When I have seen the heavens
Drawing me to peace in this life
I have also seen
The pits of hell
Burning me alive
In my flesh through my suffering
Both make me a stronger person
For without suffering
There is no growth
Without love
There is no peace
For with every compression of my lungs
I breathe new life into myself
For every form of suffering I live
Is always an opportunity for something great
For through suffering and love
Grows as a mustard seed and
Creates something called faith

PURPOSE

This is my reason to live
To try to be a testimony to everyone
For this is the day a King was born
And lived to save me from my sin
To believe is to live
To become new
To live for someone
That lived for me
It is important to celebrate You
And the day You were born
For Your life and Your ministry
Is life to everyone
And all that believe
You have changed the life of many
You are always creating and
Changing the life we live
I see You in everything You are doing
It is beautiful and perfect
The way You do things
You help me sing a new song
As if I am writing a new psalm
You are the mentor of all souls
You created everything
In Your perfect image
For we are Your peacekeepers
The representation of life
And Your story
This Christmas and forever

LAST BREATH

I have seen the day
When time ceases to exist
A breath
A last exhale
Changing physical to spiritual
Is this where the rest of my life begins
Is this my heaven
Or my own personal hell
Is this the beginning of life
When I die
Or will I die over and over again
And become a king of fire
Ruler of hell
My spirit changes
Constantly
But of all things
My spirit seeks life
For there is a glimpse
Of light in myself
But I feel like darkness changes me
I want to do good
But I feel so wicked
Now is the time to change
And become a creation of light
Before my breath stops
And I take my last breath

WORDS

Why do I write
It is the expression
Of my soul
It is the example
Flesh to paper
It is what your spirit speaks
Always from the heart
Well God bears witness to me
I lean to His words
And pray they burn into me
For words that are written
Are a living thing
The truth of one's heart
I write to show the true emotion
Of a living being
Hoping to change another's
Heart
Soul
And life
For words bring us together
Or can tear us apart
But God's living word
Will always bring us together
So be thankful
For words that are written
In love
For all things can be changed
Through words
And more powerful
God's words

CONSCIENCE

I have seen what is coming
For this is the beginning
Of the end of all humanity
Maybe I should be gone
But I am still here
Holding on to the thought
That we are lost
Holding on
I try to think heavenly
But fail constantly
I believe there is hope for us all
So I pray
I long for a better life
And maybe I should die
I have done wrong
And wrong against humanity
I deserve what I get
So since I am classified
I tend to live a peace filled life
But am mentally distraught
Damn my mind
For it is a killer, full of sin
It is paralyzing
Jesus Christ, heal my mind
So humanity is safe
For my subconscious
Wants to wage war
But my conscious wants peace
What do I do
For this is my battle
A constant war in my mind
I hope all gets well
For humanity

THANK GOD

What is the difference
Between living and death
There is a belief
That both equal the same
That there is a life after us all
For all live for a reason
And for a purpose
And try to live it
A continuous circle
A circle
A belief
That things may get better
And bring new life
The reincarnations
Of what life is
For this is the circle of life
That there is purpose
For everything we do
A belief that all is from God
I love it
How will I get through the day
For life is precious
Why do I deserve it
For this is God's glory
Mercy
Love
And I love
And I am thankful
For everything You do for me
Thank You

FOR ME NOT AGAINST ME

I believe in relationships
Even if they fall apart
To love is to live
For fear equals death
For a breath of life brings love
That is everlasting to the heart
For this is life
The hardening of hearts and
Softening of souls
The love of people brings peace
The hate of people brings fear
For what comes is everlasting
I live close to God
To show me the way
The belief that this is a new way
A cause
For mourning for someone you miss
Someone you love
Someone you believe in
I love it when people choose love
Over fear
For it might seem like all is lost

In this world
But there is always hope
Even when the world that we live in
Kills itself
I may have done it
But I believe God has it
For life is real
And I try to grip to it
I am scared to live
And sometimes scared to die
I wish I can talk
But I can't
But I have friends
That bring me peace
Thank you, Lord,
For what You do to me
For You are for me
Not against me

A GLIMPSE OF THE LIGHT TO HOLD ON

Is this the way of life
To be discontinued
To be left
And be on the march of death
Decaying in your body
And living in resentment
Is this my death march
For what is there
Out there in this life
A continuous constant of pain
My heart hurts
And feels empty
Where did my love go
I miss it
It hurts to not feel it anymore
As I once did
I feel blessed
Cause I am still here
I need to draw closer
To Jesus Christ
To feel whole again
To get close to God
So that I may stand up again
To start over and begin anew
There is still a glimpse
Of light in my heart
I am not completely lost
Let go, I am done for
I miss that love I once felt
And I want to feel it again
Thanks for life
For You are great

BEGINNING AND THE END

The bother
The thing
That eclipses my eyes
The vision that make this world
What it is
The blamer takes the blame
The erosion falters
The soul of this young man
Am I to blame
For the casualties
For the world
I don't know anymore
I wish it to be false
For the kingdom comes near
All humanity will be lost
On Earth
But not in heaven
The beginning and the end
The hope for loved ones
And humanity
A new beginning
Where I co-exist
The beginning and the end
For me

BEAUTIFUL RELIEF

I want to see what happens
Is there more out there
Than I can see
I am sure there is
For there is something
Beyond my belief
A complete roller coaster
With it's up and downs
A wild mind creating chaos
The world is beautiful
But people create problems
We worry the world
Is this our new mother
Earth
A dead world
Beyond what we can comprehend
Are we doomed
By me and my beliefs
If so I am sorry
For my intervention
For I believe there is good out there
But I am not it
Sucks to say
But I miss life as it was
The beauty and the love
I once had
It bothers me it wasn't
As it was
I am broken
Beaten down and crushed
I miss the light heartedness I had
I look forward
To my beautiful relief

THE DEMON IN ME

I have a demon in me
Something to bring me down
The fight for what is good
Or right
My purpose
What is good or right
At this point
I bring it upon myself
Am I lost
I hope not
I bring you death
The worst thing I want
Is this my cancer
Will it spread
Throughout the world

TAINTED SPIRIT

Haunted by a past
Emitted through my spirit
It is constant
The burdens it holds
And with it
The burdens to come
I hold the tears
But to release them
Might give me a moment
Of enlightenment
Hoping it will give me the strength
To move forward
I seem these days
To be more fear driven
What is going to come back
To bite me in the ass
Who is coming
And when
Where will my life go
From here
What will be my next alias
The closer that day comes
And wandering the world
In flesh
Not spirit

Death then becomes real to me now
The question is
Will I become the hunted
Or will I stay the hunter
My heart mourns
With these questions
I ask myself
For this is the life
Of someone with a little
Fallen angel blood
And who is deemed possessed
For the four horsemen have awakened
And are alive
And real
And are
On the move

BROKENHEARTED

My sadness erupts
Comprised of dry eye sockets
What is this lack of emotion
Is there a purpose
Why over the years
Have they dissipated
And left me hanging
I feel emotionless
Bound
To a broken soul
This my life
I want a blank sheet of memories
Not tainted
Swept clean of my faults
Touched by God
For my burdens keep me
In my broken state
Filling the gaps
With shit
Which keeps me from breathing
For to feel alive
Yet feel so dead
Is a man
With a broken heart

MINI-MAN

For this is the mini-man
To minimize a problem
A problem with today's society
It is so big of an effort
To make things seem smaller
For trouble comes to the man
That compiles every situation
Into the Tower of Babel
For every man that has tried
His tower has fallen
To learn a lost language
And walk his own way
To go on to see
That this life is lost
But he sees a profound life of success
But belittles his way
In which he manages his problems
For his effort to minimize his problems
He creates a bigger issue
Falling down on his face
He starts to drag his self across the ground
Till a helping hand comes
And helps him up
To open his eyes
To the truth of his problems
He then works out his problems
And in the end
Becomes a problem solver
This is the story of the mini-man
And his struggles and success
To overcome
Minimization

TO LIVE OR DIE

This is my life
And it is worth
The compromise
To not live a double life
But to live a simple life
A complex event
We all need to learn to grasp
The learning of a new skill
To bring us together
We are so different
In many aspects of life
But we are all bound
Through spiritual principles
We have all been drawn together
By God to do His will
And to help each other
For without God
Or other people
Who are we
As a human beings
How do we survive
How do we live
For years I tried to be self-reliant
Only to keep falling short
I tried to hide
In a world full of people
My thoughts
My emotions
And behaviors
Got the best of me
For to hide myself
And cut myself off
From the world

Only ended in half-measures
So I thought the bottle
To be my great escape
In this chain of events
Was the moment I thought
I can finally fit in
I started to find myself
Surrounding myself with others
Who like to do the same things
Drugs and alcohol
A little bit of smoke
A little bit of liquid courage
To get me motivated
Quickly I learned how to fall
And do the things I was doing before
But better
This was my quick descent
To my own personal hell
A life of pain and suffering

GROWING

What is the meaning of this nature
A compelling pull
A desire
Dragging me along
Into oblivion
Strong is the one
Who can stand up to it
Don't push away your weaknesses
Always prolong them
And use them to your advantage
For where there is weakness
There is opportunity to grow
Grow into a newness
Of serenity
And joy
Instead of falling on your face
And giving up on life
For we are all connected
Through our spirits and faith
We strive for more
And long to love
Or fear each other
For when we are together
We can become stronger
Through progress

Love
And knowledge
Through our strength
And weakness
For this is our community bond
Through life
The ability to live
The ability to move forward
Not backward
But focusing on the present
We do this
One day at a time
For this is the beginning
Of new life

WORDS

This is like a whisper in my ear
The sound of silence
All I can do
Is hear Your voice
It is a preference I have
To listen
And be guided
By Your spirit
Bear witness to prophecies
Told out Your lips
For they are like honey to my soul
As I follow
You become my lifeline
You become the hand I hold onto
Walking along the sandy beaches
All that is left
Is the footsteps of life
Pressed into the shoreline
Washed away
By the water of life
I belong to You
For this is the cleansing
Of my soul
For this is like a whisper
In my ear

Words written
From the sound of Your voice
Cutting into me
Like a double edged sword
The softening of a hardened heart
Pierced by words
Bringing the spiritual
To portray outward to the physical
To portray your love
Onto the world
Cause out of faith
Hope
Love
Love always perseveres
Over all

THE LADDER

This is a new sensation
A new ladder to climb
An obstacle in this life
I climb
Hanging on for dear life
This is my pinnacle
To keep climbing
To progress forward
As I climb
I begin to fear
Making it harder to progress
I hear a crack
In the ladder
The steps begin to break
And I fall backward
Down a few steps
I grip to the closest step
Fear has stuck my soul
I have not fallen back enough
To give up
My next step
Seems so far away

So I climb up
Around the obstacle
Keep on pressing forward
I am near the top now
Trying now
I press to the top
I climb over the ledge
I stand up
Worn out and beaten
And shed my skin
Cleansed of my transgressions
I am strong
And stand up on my two feet
Pressing on
To the end of the race

SITUATION ROOM

This is the situation room
To sit and decide
Between good and evil
To be pure
Cleansed through blood
Or defile yourself
And fall into your perplexed
Life of sin and be vexed
And denounce yourself
Are you fallen
Or do you rise up
Fighting demonic presences
In this fucked up world
The world is destroying itself
Because a spiritual war
Of ideologies
For everyone suffers
Trying to survive
Holding onto hope
Calling out to God
It is always this way
To try to be normal
Among the battle that wages
Between us all
God
Satan
Angels and fallen angels
They all have a presence
In this world
Fight or Fall
This is only the beginning
And this
Is our situation room

LET GO

There is a time
When all is well
Being beckoned for change
An internal hard drive
Creating neurons
In our brains
For a taste of dopamine
A release
Where is the quickest path
To escape this reality of life
Is it wrapped up in a paper
Pressed to your lips
Becoming a human smoking machine
Or is it to put the bottle
To your lips
And become a fountain of poison
And toxic waste
The change comes from attitude
Change renewing the mind
By changing the things you can
And overcoming the obstacles
That come your way
Never from a chemically induced mind
Can one change one's life
It is like pressing on a pressure point
And not releasing
All you feel is pain
For all you feel is
Shit and more shit
Yet we desire more pain
Got to let go

SINISTER

Two angels bond
To a human soul at birth
This is my first memory
After the jump
One brings upon death
The other destruction
My spirit wanders freely
Becoming notorious
In everything he does
A father signs his son over
To the government
To be examined on
And tortured
An angel abandons his comrade
With his last words
Piercing my ears
A memory not forgotten
But he today chose to be
Forgiving, for the faults
He chose to walk
A sadness fills his soul
For radical ideologies
He chose to perform
A haunting memory
For I hope the angels forgive him
For his faults
Broken in his faults
He writes these words of wisdom
For purpose
So that one day
He can stand before his men
In his weaknesses
And turn them into strengths
Pulled back up by angels
Put one foot in front of the other

And have his league stand behind him
And his commands given from above
What I need to do is rebuild my trust
And trust in His guidance
And all will come together
For Your glory
Your power
and Your kingdom
For this is a pressing matter
For all creations
It is the best means for him
To swallow his pride
And stop being the stubborn donkey
And lead his angels
And prepare for what comes next
Cause for him to be all this
And what he has been through
Has now become sinister

WRITTEN WORDS

My fingers rub
Against the roughness of the paper
Ink flows to the paper
I try to pry open my eyes
To see my thoughts come through
Onto the page
Worn body pushing itself
To write
Why do I try to write
Is it to perverse someone
Into looking into another person's thoughts
To get an opinion
Or is it just to express creativity
Or to help someone with their problems
To give a different view
For where words are written
It may cause an emotional outburst
A lingering in your mind
That illuminates a sense of joy
Therapeutic is the one
That puts his mind on the line
The ability to let out
Problem after problem
Telling the world that he struggles
The same as everyone else
For words expressed
Can always bring healing while written
Just like that love story
The BIBLE

MEDITATION

This perspiration
Contained between a blink of an eye
And a breath from the lungs
The rise and fall of the chest
That brings ecstasy to the mind
A picture formed
In your thoughts
A vision of a face
A sense of release
Bringing a peace of mind
This face gives you purpose
A sense of guidance
The voice I hear brings comfort and strength
I start to think of my faults
And how to improve them
And how can I grow from my weaknesses
And become stronger as a person
A face of a woman appears
Giving wisdom to my mind
She pushes me to become a better me
She makes me look at myself
And through her words
I begin to feel compassion and love
Helping me through my negativity
Her words of support
Help me to hold on
And press through my fears
For a man and woman
Cleanse the soul
Of a man that was broken
Tattered, torn to the brink
Of losing himself
This is my meditation

DON'T FOLLOW

I am one you do not follow
I leave my body
When my head hits the pillow
Carrying on in my endeavors
In due time I will live forever
Bringing on my vicious being
Classified are the things I've seen
Flesh punctured at the tip of my knife
Shame and guilt fill me
At the loss of life
Everyone always plays
The blame game
In the end nothing changes
And stays the same
Hear my antics
Hear my story
Through words from my voice
When I begin you will have no choice
Hear my words of spoken wisdom
To tell my story
Sometimes I can't fathom
For this is a story of broken dreams
For everything you know
Is not what it seems
For these are the dreams of sleepy hollow
For this is why
You do not follow

CREATIONS

Here I am drifting sideways
Among the ocean tides
The soothing sound
Of water crashing
Among the infinite grains of sand
Moonlight glows between the clouds
Lighting the path of my footsteps
The breeze filling my body
With a touch of coolness
In the distance
I see a mountain
And its rocky ledges
Filled with crisp white
Oxygen and snow
The beauty of this night
A moment to reflect
On how beautiful the world can really be
The purpose of its creation
Shows blatantly
Why we were given such a gift
It shows us how to survive
By pulling all things together to live
For when the winds blow
Air fills our lungs
Plants and animals survive the circle of life
We survive through every gift given freely
For this how we begin
Through the ever ending of spring
Of this life
We are what we are
Created through words
We are all a creation that gives life

CLARITY

There is a pause in my breath
A moment
A thought
An instant of clarity
What will push me to my brink
Is it the circumstances
That are holding me back
Blocked by my situation
Is it my emotions
Ready to explode at any moment
Is it my thoughts
Running like a rampage
Through my mind
I watch and learn
To see
How I respond
To see
My behavior
At the response of my beliefs
A kind jester
Makes you respond
With what emotion
How you feel that day
Can also be the difference
Of your behavior
The thought of motivation
Is compelling
Becoming a positive

Not escalating into a behavior
That brings me down
And someone else
For this is my moment
The thought
And there is my clarity
A belief
That everything you think
Is always thought about
Before it hits your consciousness
Pushing to your conscious memory
Add in response through emotion
And inevitability in a behavior
For all things start
With a thought
And build from there

HOW I MET THE QUEEN OF THE CARTEL

This is the becoming of a new age
This is the age where time stands still
For 33 years
I have accomplished
Everything imaginable
33 was the age
In which I came into this world
Born I was 0
In spirit I was 33
Shapeshifting into a poor man
I first saw her beauty
From across the crowds
In the Mexican market
Carrying her basket of flowers
I walked up to her
Spoke nervously as a smile persists
A thought of interest
I then asked her
To come have something to eat
We sit laughing
Smile
Caught up in our jokes
Exchanging words
I never felt this before
As the first ounce of love hits my heart
I then
Being a gentleman
And we talk and conversate
All the way to her house

I look her in the eye
And move my head in
And go for the kiss
With pressed lips
Electricity strikes my body
And I pull her close
As our lips separate
I am greeted with a smile
She looks down blushing
And with her fingers
Brushes her hair back behind her ear
Spoken words of the night end
Fill my plush lips
As I say goodnight
And I will find you tomorrow
I start to walk away
And her face is an image to my eyes
I turn and look
Twice
For her beauty ignites the night
And she smiles and fades
Behind the closed door

FEAR OF ME

Fear
The emotion
Overtaking me
The emotion
Given to me
Through my scars
And emitted by my past
For it's shown through my inability
To tell my story
For my experiences
Can be too much for me to take
What about for the people I tell
What will they think of me
Will they whisper
Behind my back
Spreading my craziness
Throughout this place
For I don't want to be stuck
To deal with it
So vulnerable
I feel weak
For not saying what is going on
I feel a deep doubt
An empty hole
In my stomach
Surrounded by butterflies
Scared of myself
And what I am capable of doing
I feel I am
A destructive entity
And am scared of purpose

These are the thoughts
That haunt me
I feel pulled in another direction
Where do I go from here
What is the cause of this purpose
To walk my life in fear
Till my fears are overcome
Shaking in my skin
I need to push myself
To express my emotions
And overcome my fear
To talk about myself
My fear might dissipate
For behind my sense of fear
Is a story that needs told
For a healing heart and mind

SURRENDER TO SUBMIT

We must surrender
To submit
To the circumstances
That compile
Into a double-mind mentality
For to submit
Before you surrender
Only results in half measures
For the battle that wages within
Between my conscious
And my subconscious
Is fierce
Like a marauder
Hitting me with thoughts
For is it first thought no
Or is it first thought wrong
What will entice
My next thought or action
What memory
Is going to bring my next emotion
For when I surrender these moments
A piece of me releases the stone
Which is holding me under water
I can now breathe again
And submit
To the knowledge
Learned from experience
Placed into action

My willingness prevails
Keying and replacing
The old with the new
For when you look inside
Don't let your past experiences
Cause you horror
But turn these experiences
Into a new creation
And learn
And grow
Strengthening who you are
And creating new memories
For when you surrender
It is always easier to submit
To new life

YOU ARE ALWAYS MISSED

Today I took a moment
To think of you
How much joy came to me
A simple text
Puts a smile to my face
I put a spot in my memory for you
Cause you are worth every brain cell to me
You are the person
That is always there
Cause I can't stop thinking of you
I remember the memories
Of the happiness we have
Your crazy bucket list
The times I would take a bullet for you
The times with fashion
And with fame
And most of all
Our kids
And our faith in God
These things are important
And I am trying to gain ground
Make up for my mistakes
For what has happened
Has ripped my soul apart
For when you hurt
I am only hurting myself
For I still fill my heart

With love for you
To see that smile
To hear your voice
And what is going on with you
For to me you are
My best friend
And I am grateful for every moment
I get to spend with you
So thank you
And my loves goes out to you
To help you through
Every aspect of your life
Love you so much

COMMUNICATION

Thank you, Savanah
For to hear from you
Lightens the weight
Of the problems
That are bestowed upon me
A moment to wind down
And a time to vent
And release a part of myself to you
For you to reach out
And be worried
I am grateful
For I tend to worry about myself
Telling you some of my secrets
Was nerve wracking
Which is why I was laughing
Cause I was scared to tell you
Some of those secrets
I put myself out there
Cause I trust you
And I know our conversations
Are between us
Unless I write about it
For to hear from you
Brings joy to this man
Being built up and not torn down
A spoken word straight from your mouth
With a full hearted response
Goes a long way
So I thank you again, cousin
For a text and a phone call
To be the highlight of my day

PORTRAIT

This is the end of a cool crisp winter
Oxygen fills the air
A freshness fills the blue skies
This is a bleak memory of my past
Cause in my future
I sit in green pastures
Watching the wind blow the brush
Moving with every swoosh
The leaves bloom and bring life to the trees
Bringing life to living organisms
For where does the wind stop
It is a continuous cycle
That stretches across the world
A life force pressing against my flesh
Giving off a life force
Giving me energy
For in the present
I sit in dryness inside
Hidden from the weather
Learning about the emotional
Physical
Spiritual
Aspects of life
The sun shining through the window
For it gives life to myself and peers
It's rays giving sight
And colors to the eyes
Reflecting life
Revealing itself before us
This is what life brings us
A beautiful picture portrait before us
The perfect portrait

TAKE CONTROL

This is my purpose
To change into the person
Jesus wants me to be
A purpose which changes
At a moment's notice
For where there is purpose
There is always the willingness
To give control over
To the care of God
For there is always the opportunity
To grow in your relationship
with Him
He never ceases to show you the path
In which to walk
Do not be swallowed
By your past
And turn to God and
He will wash the slate clean
For it is not accepting
God's forgiveness
That is the problem
It is inevitably accepting
forgiveness of oneself
And facing yourself
For healing does not happen overnight
But happens
Over a lifetime

For Your love is sufficient for me
in every way
So guide my spirit back home
By taking control
Cause I tried this myself
And I believe
You are the solution
Not the problem
I have become an issue
Because my pride
Is getting in the way
And I was driving drunk
In my own arrogance
To see exactly what You wanted me to do
So take control of my bus
And drive me back home
to You
God

THE AWAKENING

Here I am
Fighting with my memories
The past flashing before my eyes
It seems like a constant attack
On myself and my self-worth
Tearing down my walls
I have presented myself
Vulnerable
Hurting for my mistakes
I hold on
To show who I am
Can bring a paralyzing fear
To beckon me to run
From the person I have become
Over the years
I shouldn't let my transgressions
Stop me from progression
I should face my burdens
One by one
I should just say
What is on my heart
For it can save someone's soul
I know there is a lot to learn
From past experiences
But I cannot let the past
Control what the future holds
For there is a lot to live for
And my fears are holding me back

How do I move forward
Changing into the person I am to become
I need a life changing experience
The great awakening
Of mind
Of body
And of soul
To move and become
The ever changing me
Always open
Always knocking
Looking for answers
For every answer
Can be a chance to respond
To the new becoming
Of my resurrection to life

BECOMING

In the beginning
You usually start out
With childhood innocence
Learning from the moment
Life is given
Usually move forward
To innocence
To victim
To the cause of problem
(The predator)
For when you learn
From someone
Your whole life
A part of that person
Stays with you
It then becomes you
To change the behaviors learned
As is guided through Your spirit
For God will take your character defects
Teach you to wield them
For the better good
Of those you meet
So now you become the teacher
Yet still open to new ideas
Do not stick your head in the dirt
And close your eyes off from the world
Embrace everything
And everyone
For your story can change someone

To change the world
Be a helping hand to the lost
And confront them with love
Etching truth into the heart of man
Be the one to lead them
Keep them safe
Don't throw them away
Listen to the words of truth
And begin your ministry
Not forgetting where you came from
And remembering who you are
And who you are to become

ACCEPTING WILLINGLY

By dwelling on my willfulness
Am I thinking about forfeiting
All willingness
Why do I struggle with things
As radical acceptance
For being willing
Is one of the first steps
To accepting the terms
In which life measures out to you
In paving the path of serenity
Live in the moment
For what comes next
Might be that moment
Which may be the hardest to accept
And willingness
Just might paint
That picture of what ifs
For to overthink can make
Or break you
And how you proceed through life
So have the willingness
To open the pages of life
Written like a script
And build your house upon the rock
For a steady foundation
And upon all willingness

Reach out
Climb over your obstacles
Till one breathes that last breath
For the faith .
Which is bestowed upon your life
Will help make life fulfilling
Not just a half full cup of wine
Feeding an empty soul
For the prospects of all life
Can be that first step
Of acceptance
As you take that first step
Of willingness
And grasping a spiritual life
Sounds a little like
Freedom

BATTLING CHEMICAL REACTION

There is the belief
That there is something out there
Pushing your trigger points
A simple urge
Pressed into the mind
Compelling you to the brink
Of a simple dose of medication
It tugs
And presses your very soul
Into despair
The battle wages on
With open pores and moist skin
I begin to shake
Body aching
My urges rage through
Thought to thought
Cycling
Through my mind
I want more
My brain tell me
With an upside down smile
I begin to reflect
What is my biggest problem
With this day
Is this me being hungry
Angry
Lonely and tired

The 4 things that can bring me back
To destroying my vessel
Tearing down my temple
For these are my times
Of temptation
The wanting of chemicals
To alter my world
So I don't have to think
Of this reality
That is mine
So I question my thoughts
And challenge the memory
That attacks me
How, God, do I deal
With the issues probing
Tearing at my nerves
So I don't pick up my liquid poison
My empty soul
How do I fill back up my spirit
For I am longing for more of You
So I don't go back
To my old self
And my days of disgrace

WORKING IT OUT

Praise be to the Lord Almighty
For when anger strikes
This can be the collapse
Of your resolve
Problems building
Stacked around
Like shit piled up
And you are stuck
In your resentments
Fuming
You hold on to things
That you carry to the next life
Questioned by God
For the reasoning
Behind not being able to let go
I stand before God
But my reasoning
Only seems senile
For the anger that erupted
Still lingers
And the shame that follows
Fills me with thoughts of my issues
God asks me
Deal with your resentments
And thanks me for coming to Him
With an honest heart
Don't let your resentments
Become the thing
That tears you away from Me

But let them be the things that fulfill
What I have for you
For life is My gift to you
Don't tarnish it
Stay close to Me
Drawing near to Me
For I only offer life
In great abundance
So let go
Of what resentments you have
And forgive
Pray for the person
That is taking away your joy
Of all else place your trust in Me
For God wants you to have freedom
And He will always
Be calling your name

LIFE AND THE MIND

A peace of mind
With a quick spoken word
The words that flip off the tongue
Strike like a serpent
Among feelings
There is woe
A feeling inside
That irks my soul
This is sorrow
An inner condemnation
The first sign of shame
The belief
That I did something wrong
And I am not good enough
Crosses my thoughts
Anger peaks
The tip of the iceberg
To climb back down
Could bring conviction
For looking through my emotions
To clear my faults
To find a solution
And make amends
To look through the eyes
And opinions of another
To be done with this anger
Don't let the sun go down
And hold these feelings
For tomorrow is a new day
And you can get your freedom

From what is holding you back
For your belief system
Can lead your ways
Or wake up
And have a horrible day
So deal with the problems
We have today
For if you don't
Your joy can be taken away
For simple minded is the one
Who deals with their thoughts
And emotions
Becoming a compelling force
To change their self and others
Approach in love
And change
And fix everything you can
Before your mind tears your life apart
To sum this up
Live a balanced life

OPENING

My sense of release
Spoken from honest words
The breaking of chains
Binding me
Start to unlink a bondage
That has been locked up
I now have found a key
The thoughts
That have been haunting myself
I now feel compelled to say more
For a voice spoken
Might change someone's outlook
A change of perception
A transforming of the mind
For I have been bound
By my feelings
And what people might think
A sense of fear
I put myself
Into a vulnerable spot today
The opening of my heart
Brought discomfort
But brought some peace
To this human
Who fights with himself every day
The fight still continues

But to be an open book
Is not weakness
But provides a path to grow
Strengthen
And brings upon one less thing
To bind you into your past
For this is my escape route
My freedom
And my validation
In life
To release
And be fulfilling
Through an open mouth

SCHIZO

This is the life and mind
Of a Schizophrenic
To see the future
But can I change it
The ability to look back
And see yourself
Before birth
Living in the heavens
Jumping down
And being put
In this wretched human body
For when I watch the news
I have to see
What I am doing to this world
I am so ashamed of who I am
The barrage of air strikes
The violence
I blame myself
For the world's problems
For I know I am being watched
Listened in on
By a wire-tap
Speaking through my TV
To the world
And it's leaders
Telling them
What is in hand for them

The panic
The anxiety
And the fear
Consumes me
Wondering
Why they haven't come for me
And ended me
Are people scared of who I am
And what I am capable of
For I am the reincarnation
Of King David
Ruler of Israel
I am the harbinger of Death
One of the 4 horsemen
And I am Satan's son
The Antichrist
I learn to deal with these thoughts
And what I have done
For if all else fails
God
Please
Save me

AT THE QUEENS DEFENSE

This is a compelling story
Of a woman
An instant in which
She had to save herself
She walks into her room
Within her villa
A beautiful
Well decorated room
Of a queen
Her henchmen come in
And sense her king is gone
Faded away
And gone out of her life
Her henchmen start to suggest
Sexual interest
A wicked smile
Comes off the faces of her men
In her vulnerability
She fights to save herself
They push her onto the bed
And begin
To try to rape
I stand there
With a gun in my hand
Gun pointed
At the henchmen
And ready to squeeze the trigger
No one knows
That I am there
So angry
I am in tears
Wanting to take their lives
I tell her
To take the gun out of their holster
And shoot them

Ready to shoot
I hold back
So she can become
The person she is today
Quickly she grabs the gun
And three shots ring out
And now 3 dead bodies
Fall onto her
Tears fall down her face
The fear in her eyes
Piercing me
I tell myself
This is her training
To be able to stand up
And defend herself
Among her men
I disappear
Knowing she is going to be alright
Back into my human body
Sadness
For having to put her into this situation
For I am proud of her
For what she did
For this is her training ground
The start
Of the person she is today

LOOKING IN THE MIRROR

I am here sitting
Learning how to live life to its fullest
To face my resentments
And forgive myself and others
I am to engage into a past
And confront the realities of life
It is a continuous cycle
Of dealing with emotions
Sadness fills my body
To look backward
To learn who I am
How do I deal with this
How can I learn
From my experiences
Will I come face to face
With myself
And look in the mirror
To see the true identity
Of who I am
It is hard
To look myself in the eye
And peer into my soul
To fight back
What holds me back
My intellect fights the urge to run
Pushing through my past
My thoughts and emotions
Send out mixed messages

I confront
And push through the barriers
Overcoming
Yet worn down
I pray
Ask for help
Through my own illness
I am weak
Beaten down
From my situation
Now
Because of my faith
I can now move forward in life
I now focus
Not on my eyes
But who I am
I smile now
Because now
I can accept who I am
Look into my soul
Into the mirror
And know
I am not the old me
And live in peace
And be joyful
Amongst the chaos

GONE BOY, GONE

This is my land
A place of benevolence
I sit with my gun in hand
I wait for my enemies to come for me
Paranoid
I am in a constant state of emergency
The phone rings and I jump
I walk over
And hear the sound of a click
As I answer the phone
Who are you, I ask
A voice answers
But won't give a name
He gives a warning
That something is coming
And that I should be prepared
For what is to come next
Nervously I accept his warning
And put the phone down
I cry
Tear drops run down my face
Fear ridden
My lungs push breath out my lungs
Heavily
My heart pounding
Blood pressure rising
I break out in hives and itch radically
Redness comes to my skin
I hear the doorbell and walk softly
So the person on the other end of the door
Doesn't hear me

I place my face closer to the door
And look through the peep hole
I see a woman I once knew
A beauty
For I know what she is capable of doing
I open the door
And she disappears before my eyes
What is going on, I ask myself
All the best memories of her
Rush back to my memory
And knowing wherever she is
She is ok
Brings joy
I calm myself
Sitting
Putting a cigarette to my lips
Smiling
Look up
And see a glimmer from the bushes
I hear the sound of a rifle shot
And I feel the pressure
Of the bullet to my forehead
As my life erases
Into the darkness
I fall into the deepest sleep
Known as death

2001

In the year 2001
In Bagdad
I see the bombs drop
And see people and buildings crumble
I walk the streets
Preparing myself for battle
I see my target
And the beast overtakes me
I run through the city
Chasing the leader
I pull out my gun
And start shooting
Shot after shot
Fired
I watch as
Men
Women
And children
Fall
Taking out some of his men
His leaders
Also start to scatter
In fear
Some no longer fight
And run
Some fought
And died
Each leader that survived
Was put to a playing card
I then pull out my knife
And put quick end to them
The memory
Of the barrage of bullets
And the memory
Of slit throats

I remember that child
The beast stopped
And gave me back my conscience
I look down
And see
A little girl in fear
I look around
Seeing the carnage
And I made the conscious decision
To cut her throat
Then I lost consciousness
And with rigid teeth
Looked their leader in the face
I start chasing him
Again
Out to get him
Distracted
I turn to chase
One of his leaders
And I take another
But with this in mind
The leader of Iraq escapes
And is now in hiding
And his leaders
Hiding from the deployment
About to enter Bagdad
For this is the raid that took place
Before the troops arrived
3000+ people died that day
And this is the history
No one knows

DEBBIE-DOWNER

Why am I feeling down today
I sit because I had to be that honest
With my mom
Open up with her about
What is going on in my mind
Is it me trying to ask for help
But the words
Won't come out my mouth
I feel like isolating
Concealing myself
I feel like everything I plan
Is put down and shit on
As of right now
I am not a baby
I can be responsible
To be told
I might have to be on Social Security
I think insults my intelligence
I might have a disease
But it doesn't mean
To belittle
Every aspect of life
Let me make a decision
And quit making decisions
For me
It vexes me
I do agree

I need to get off overnights
Cause I hate the broken record
Playing in my mind
My negativity today
Is bringing me down
So not to be a hum-bug
For this is my day
Today
And I apologize
For my frustrations
And that my writing
Is not positive
But tomorrow is a new day
And I know what was said
Are options

CONVERSATIONS

A sense of relief
Falls over me
When someone sits down
To let me vent
And let go
A welcoming face
Lets me inspire him
It hits his heart and
Brings me to smile
His words
His wisdom
And him lending me a helping hand
His understanding of things
Made me feel comfortable
And I let him into my mind
It's the hardest thing to do
Along came another friend
Come lifting me up
Put me in my spot
Telling me
Not to beat myself up
Just like the last friend
He made me look at the positive
And made me challenge
My negative thoughts
Another smile comes to me
For I know I am caught

In that broken record mentality
Rapid thoughts
Too much dopamine
Bringing me down
But because of my friends
I can go to bed
With my anxiety down
And my frustrations
Withering away
For without others
I would be lost
And be wondering
What is the point
If there is no one
There are others
Who keep me on my two feet
So, Thank You!

THE HANGING OF KING

I stand amongst the crowds
The screams and yells of his people
Discriminate against him
The soldiers stand there
Preparing for his demise
At attention he stands
With pride
With fear in his eyes
Breathing heavily
As his time grows near
A leader stands on the wooden floor
That would
In due time
Lead to his last breath
I walk up
And put the black bag over his face
I walk around to his back
And whisper into his ear
And tell him
He is going to have to take one
For the team
Sorrow entices him
Tears
Heavy breathing
And words of forgiveness come out
I walk down the wooden steps
Toward the lever
That will feed him

His last breath
As he speaks his last word
I pull the lever
The floor falls
Beneath his feet
I stand with a crooked smile
As I jump back into formation
I see his nerves go into shock
Body shaking
This a man
Framed for the 3000+ that died
At the beginning of a war
For I lost something that day
A part of me also died that day
For he was someone
I once called friend

PRINTED HEART

I speak openly with a king
Tell him that I pull the strings
Of the government
I send him a war message
Preparing for the worst
A couple days later
Artillery falls down upon South Korea
A few good men die
People survive
The continuous barrage of shells
Part of my message was
You will die if you attack
I send in the cavalry
And we prepare for wargames
They give the warning shot
Saying our wargames
Are going to start a war
They go before China
And they are put in their spot
Their leader walks out scared
And looks like a stick up his ass
And the South laughs in his face
In the mean while
They give us 2 more warning shots
Pushing us further South
Then back to Japan
Then they threaten to shoot off nukes
We back off completely

Later I fall asleep
And I lean
Crouched at the end of his bed
A conversation between him and I
I told you
I would kill you
If you attack the South
He says that he knows
I tell him how bad a leader he is
And he doesn't care about his people
I then ask him
If he is ready to go
And he answers yes
I place my hand through his chest
And grip his heart
Burning my hand print
Into his heart
I look at the blank stare in his eyes
As life dissipates from his body
I close his eyes
And disappear
Back into my body
I wake up
Go to work
And hear that he died in his sleep
When the autopsy came out
My hand print was burned
Into his heart

GOODBYE, GLADICE

This is my time
Of sorrow
A time when I experience
The loss of a loved one
For God gave her a life
And in time
Has finished her race
There were times of joy
Where your smile
Lit up the room
Times you would take the time
And sit beside me
And fish with me
And talk
The joy you brought
To my heart
Still lingers
You are not gone
You are still alive to me
For the memories you gave me
Make you alive
Till the day I die
I pray for your safe passage
To heaven
And you can walk
Hand in hand
With Jesus
And your husband

I am sad
That you are no longer here
Your suffering
Has now stopped
May peace be with you
I am sorry
I can't be at your funeral
But I am trying to get better
It frustrates me
Cause I want to celebrate
Your great life here on Earth
And I want you to know
I love you and
Goodbye, Gladice

HELPING HAND

When I place my head
Upon that pillow
I hear the sounds of string instruments
Like the Cello
The sound of melody
Erupts in my ears
Painting a picture
Of someone near
I look to see
A woman with a kindle
To see a spider
Web it's spindle
I feel the tears
That drip down my face
As I fall to my knees
To face disgrace
This feeling of shame
I try to embrace
For is this my medication
I can taste
She reaches down
With an open palm
For are you the woman
I write about in psalms
There is fear
To take her hand
For I feel I should die
In this sinking sand
For I have harmed you

So why help
For God has sent me
To help this whelp
I sense forgiveness
In her heart
So I take God's blessing
Though I feel dark
For me to deny her
Would not be smart
The hand grips my hand
To pull me from the shadows
To the light
The path in which I wallow
Strangeness follows
With a sigh of relief
For this woman
Sent by God
Brought me to belief
Forgiveness goes a long way
When you let go
Cause an act of kindness
Can make this so

DEATH'S CURTAIN

Is this what someone looks like
With certain death
Does the curtain fall
For everyone to see
For this is the moment
Of sunken eyes and
The greatest of all
Fear
Lingers
Throughout your entire body
You look to see
A glimpse of yourself
And the past ignites
Before your eyes
Displaying your story
Right in front of you
The good
The bad
And the ugly
Your memories
Portray to you the real you
The concepts of who you are
Take a turn
And hit you
With your own personal hell
Is this a taste of luxury
Are these the demons
That taunted me my whole life
For my ability to fit in
Is the very thing
That betrayed my trust

The longing for normality
Is the thing
That brought me to this fatality
A moment
A last breath
And then I disappear
From this materialistic world
Is this my way
Of saying good-bye
To this lost soul
I have become
And seeking out a new life
In which life
Becomes worth living
And dying
To see my old self
To bring my soul back
To spiritual principles
And take that kiss of death
To go on
And fly again

REBUTTAL

This is the rebuttal
To last night's poem
For I am sorry
For making your hearts worry
About this soul
For death was not my reasoning
Behind those written words
It was to tell you
About a time I was lost
And the emotions
And thoughts
That were running through my head
For I lost 7 years of life
For my mistakes
For there was I time
I did want to be 6 ft. under
I tried 9 times
And 3 others with assistance
Only for the gun I had
To not go off
Every time
I am actually very content
With life right now
This is because
The mercy and grace
Of my lord, Jesus Christ
He denied me death
And in return gave me life
For this is my time
Of cleansing
And He gave me a new season

Life is now precious to me
And I am grateful
For every day He gives me
This is His love story to me
To not let go
And to follow Him
For life will be given to you
In abundance
Life is my gift to you, He said
This is why I keep telling you
No
You're not done yet
So I listen
For His voice to guide
And lead me
Upon the green pastures

LETTER TO A FRIEND

If you get this
We want you to know
That we are worried about you
For you are a part of our group
And we need you here
We sit and reminisce
About how to help
You
Your knowledge and opinion
Matter to us
I need to hear your story
Because you are an inspiration to us
So please
Put the party on hold
And go home to your parents
They stopped here today
Looking for you
Their love shows
Through their actions
They will keep searching
Do what you said
You were going to do
Put yourself into inpatient
And get the help you need

Quit running
From yourself
And confront who you are
We want you better
Quit looking in the mirror
And hating yourself
For what I saw
Was not a monster
But I saw a champion
A winner
So don't give up
But fix yourself
And come back
To the people that care

BE PATIENT

This is what I want
A quick fix
Sometimes I wish a doctor
Would cut open my skull
Remove my brain
And replace it
With a baby's brain
To grow and start anew
This is a problem
With myself
And I am always looking
For that quick gratification
I would not be
Who I am today
Without my past experiences
I keep looking
Deeper and deeper
Searching for the answers
For I am grateful
For what God shows me
We have to fix ourselves
Day by day
Sometimes moment by moment
So I pray to Jesus
To guide my day
And for the power to do His will
To fix oneself
Takes a lifetime
For we took a lifetime to mess it up
So quit looking for that
Quick fix
And ask for a little bit
Of Patience

RAPED

Blessed our those
That are down trodden
For to be down is always the way
To pick yourself back up
For those like me
Raped
Of my innocence
I express thanks
And am grateful
I am saved
By grace
May mercy fall upon the hands
That touched this soul
Still caught in my memories
Of those that brought harm
I am here today
Learning to grow
Learning to teach
Reaching out today
With forgiveness in my heart
For to sit here and hate
Is only going to stop me in my tracks
And keep me from moving forward
The memory hurts
But my experiences
Are there to help others
How to deal with their issues
For the blessing comes from God
And through the lives you save
For blessed are those
That are down trodden
And learn from the things
That raped you.

CHANGE OF HEART

This is the place
Where my feelings follow
This place I beckon to go
I long for it
But am so far
From reaching it
How does one get to the place
He wants to be
Do you set the goal
And might
One day
Get there
For this is my story
Of my long trudge home
A story of life
To excel
And fall on my face
Was once comfortable to me
For I was touched by an angel
Who led me to my Father
A simple taste of grace
Upon my taste buds
A little mercy
To pick me up off my face
So that I can clean the mud off my face
To grow in my faith
He called me son
And gave me a new life
So that He can strengthen me
To grow like a mustard seed
For what might seem small
Will always grow

To outweigh the odds
He takes His hand
Molding my heart
Taking away my cold heart
Gradually softening my soul
My instinct tells me
That this is the change
I need to experience
The taking on a new form
Of myself
To tell my story
Of the one who saves
And is ever changing
The ones He loves
So He took my hand
And He guides me
Through life
Step by step
Till my heart seizes
And I carry on
To the next step of life

FALL TO RISE

The pride of man
Was the collapse of the world
Two humans deceived by the serpent
To eat
From the tree of good and evil
The tree of life
Protected
By flames of a blade
We fell and died that day
Cursed
We were banished from the garden
Put to labor and child bearing
To survive
But God did not leave us
He led us
To who we are today as people
Still giving him praise
For every creation does
For the world flourished
Because He never left us
To be alone
To fend for ourselves
He created woman
From a rib bone
As a man slept
So that life shall prevail

On this planet
For when all mankind fell
God's presence is still here
Guiding the steps of man
According to His purpose
For to die to flesh
Is always the way
To allow God to bear witness
And lead your spirit
Back to eat the fruit
From the tree of life
For from dust we came
To dust we will return
But in spirit to life
Goes on forever

WAYWARD TO CHRIST

I wander wayward
Through the tunnels
Of my destiny
I begin to think to myself
Where am I going
Am I coming to my destination soon
For I feel fear
For I have no idea
What waits at the end
My conscious
Filled with the unknown
Creeping in on me
I then reach a door
And open it
And walk through it
All of a sudden
My demons jump on my back
Weighing me down to the ground
Taking bits of my flesh
I put my hand out
And they take my hand
And one bites into my wrist
They jump on me more
And take
Bite after bite
Till I lay there
A bare skeleton
Is this what my life holds
To be beaten
And eaten
By my demons

No
I believe not
Because it is Jesus Christ's blood
Spilt at the cross
For me
That cleans my slate
And give me life
In abundance
He is the strength
Given to overcome
Life's problems
Through Him
That doesn't let
The devil control my life
For if God is with you
Who can be against you
For my faith
Might lead me into hard decisions
Ask for guidance
And it is given freely
For Jesus takes this wicked man
And makes him righteous
In the sight of man
For He is always
Where you are

INSPIRATION

There is a man
Sitting writing
A letter of love to others
His words
Touch the souls of men
I once called him mentor
And today what Christ does
Through him
Is still teaching the ways of God
Blessed is this man
For he has been humble
In all areas of his life
For God's wisdom
Flows out of him
Changing everyone he meets
This is my thanks to God
For allowing Jesus
To use this man in my life years
Allow him to teach
And improve
Who I have become
Him
Like me
We are the ragamuffins
In which Jesus helped stand
On solid ground
To keep our feet steady
Beloved are the ones
Who keep close to what holds still

Jesus tells me that
Is that hope
That ray of light
He placed there
To lead
And become
An inspiration to me
Cause this is a story
Of what I think of you
Jesus, continue to bless this man
Who took years
To build me through you
He is still
To this day
My inspiration from you, God
I will stay still
And walk your path
To the days of my life have passed
And so will he.

BOOK TWO

GOD'S SPOKEN WISDOM

Through the voice of God
I exist
Every word spoken
Every breath taken
Formed from words
I walk the path spoken to me
Always surrounded
By words that keep us going
God shows love
In every word
Spoken from His lips
His words touch
Every part of life
And gives to us
Through His spirit
The epitome of wisdom
Words can be the thing
That changes a man
Into the person
God wants him to be
A real champion
Given wisdom
To place life
In another human being
Through the presence
Of Jesus Christ
In us
His words flow
When the spirit of God
Moves through us

To teach others of His glory
For the world
Spoken to life
We learned to survive
By words
For all things exist
Through God
Cause He spoke it
Into existence
That is how I am here
On this planet
For a purpose
By God's wisdom
For the breath of life
Gave birth to everything
So speak in love
And love your neighbor
As you love yourself
For the words you speak
Should always
Give God the glory He deserves

CHECK THE FACTS

Here I am
Reminiscing
About how angry I was
With my mom
Over nothing
The worst thoughts
Running through my head
Thinking she
Was going to try
And control my project
Selfish
I was being all day
I was complaining
And letting it get to my head
I talked to at least 6
7 different sources
About what I thought she was doing
I could not stop
The racing thoughts
Running through my head
No matter what I would do
I came home
And read my Bible
And learning about the struggles
God's people went through
And how they had the faith to do
What God had told
And how they trusted Him

So I prayed
And began to lay my burden
Onto Jesus Christ
What fruits of the spirit
Do I want to apply to my life
I ask myself
Prayed for all of them
So I can become more Christlike
I then went to bed
And laid
And talked to God
He told me to hear
What my mother had to say
So I slept
And woke up
And had a conversation
She said she wanted to edit
And retype some of the pages
In my writings
I felt relieved
But stupid
Cause I was not patient
And lay down my burden
Onto God
Right away
My joy was taken away
Cause I didn't check the facts.

WEIGHED DOWN

I can feel the whirlwind
On my fingertips
The wanting of Love
In my heart
The cello plays
As my soul cries
My heart changes
While the tide rises
And the waves crush my self-esteem
There is this yearning
The want to belong
The want to be accepted
For who I am
I know I am different
But there are the similarities
Between us all
I am sorry for the way
I see the world
I am scared
Of the rejection of people
For I am dependent upon them
For the survival
Of my spiritual ambitions
For my heart cries out
For their help
May not my guilt
And shame
Level me out
For to pull the face from the angel
Could bring my walls
Crumbling down
I must stand strong

When trials weigh me down
Not through my own
But God's strength
Is stronger than my self-will
I am tired of my self-pity
Fear seems to be driving me
At the moment
I am hurt by my own ambition
And it is only hurting others
As my anger erupts
For I am an emotional mess
Grieving for my losses
Is this my tyranny
That my soul explodes
With emotion
And I disappear
There is hope
Love
And faith
All of which keep me going
I know though
Deep down
I can't live
Without the love of others
And mostly God's love
Help me love myself right now
And put aside my depression

JOY THROUGH JESUS

Joy overflows
Out of me
Still overwhelmed
By the world
I look to the skies
A prayer of gratitude
Comes to mind
A simple thank you
To Jesus
For all He is doing
In and through me
Compels me
To be filled up spiritually
For the people He touches
Through this weakened body
Of flesh and bone
Are touched by Your spirit
Guiding them closer
To Your presence
Bringing them to tears
As broken as we come
The healing begins
For God touches
And works
Through the weak
And causes them to grow
In their faith in Him
And gives hope
To those brought down
By the things of this world
There is always a hand

Held out to you
Will you leave it hanging
Or will you take it
And walk in the love
Of Jesus Christ
Will you walk through the door
He has opened for you
For God's wisdom
Is gained through knowledge
And experiences He puts in front of you
For to know God
Brings you into a relationship with Him
Then the flood gates open
And you are filled
With the Spirit
And when hard times hit
There is much joy
To fill the gaps

LETTER TO A FRIEND

Is this my epiphany
To be overcome
With mental problems
And tossing pills down my throat
The memories seem very real
To me
A version of myself
Clothed in the blood of others
Losing people that are close
Hurts
But letting them go
Is harder
All I wanted
Was to be accepted
But my illness corrupted that
I still love
But am not in love
With you
Just the mirrored version
Of yourself
Hard to explain
For these memories
Might be part
Of my mental disorder
I still want to be
Part of your life
A good friend
Not one
That scares you away
One that is there to help
In times of need

I do miss hanging out
I hope to do it again
Someday
I ask
For a change of heart
And not to treat me
Differently than before
For my struggles with life
Run deep
And are hard for me to bear
I hope you read this
And I hope you understand
That I am going to probably still struggle
Mentally
With my condition
And I hope you can help
When I am
I do miss you
And I hope you are doing well
Just be careful of the situations
You get yourself into
You can talk to me anytime
Cause you are a great friend

THE HEART

I hear a beating heart
I look toward it
To see tears of blood
This represents my sorrow
I watch as my heart
Sinks and stops
For a sec
As I grieve for my losses
But my heart still pounds
I fall to my knees
In prayer
And my heart pounds
Faster and faster
Help me Lord
For I have failed again
Take this grief and sorrow
And please take it from me
The heart stops pounding
And I see it begin to crack
And watch as it starts to crumble
Turning to dust
As it hits the ground
Lord, I am so broken
Please help me
Fix this heart
For I know it is not my time yet
To return to the dust

So Jesus puts His hand
To my chest
And calmness overcomes me
As my heart heals
I watch the dust rise
Changing back
Into the figure of a heart
Is this my healing
And I give thanks
To the high King
My Savior
From the issues that rise
From the world view situations
Love then finds me
And a halo rises
Above the heart
This is me
Turning my trust over to God
My heart no longer grieves
Or is filled with sorrow
For God's love is profound
In every way
And turned my heart to Him

PRAISE AMONGST THE STRUGGLES

Today has made me exuberant
I am very accomplished today
It was non-stop things to do
I am still finding out
More about myself
I now have the energy to do
What is put to my mind
At the moment
Not procrastinating
But doing God's will for the day
I went to find myself today
Went to the doctors
And found out my diagnosis
For I have hit a low
With my meds
They seem to not be working
And I have scared people
This is my struggle right now
To overcome
My chemical imbalance
In my brain
So I talk
About how my mental illness
And my addiction
Can lead me back to using
So I called a friend
And sought prayer
We prayed

For the wisdom to know what to do
And I also sought out God's wisdom
I went to work
Struggled with my thoughts
And as I walked out
People gave me praise
For my hard work
Thank you, Jesus, for this day
Cause with it's struggles
You were there
And You deserve praise
I went over to my friend's house
To tell them my day
I must really be
The beloved of Jesus Christ
For all I received
Was love
From everyone

PAVE THE WAY

Sometimes things
Are not what they seem
For the memories remain
Of angels
Heaven
And God
The purpose
We were sent down here for
The path seems unclear
How do I fulfill the purpose
In which God gave me
To pave the way
Of the coming of Jesus Christ
Give me vision, Lord
To the next steps
To fulfill Your will
I have this moment
Right here
Right now
I come to You
To help fulfill Your prophecies
Leading me back to You, Lord
For Your word
Has set my spirit on fire
For You
Taking the hammer
and crushing my transgressions
Of this day
The morning
Has been a time of renewal
To be still
And relax in Your presence

Thank You, Lord
For my oar back
For I paddle through the trials of life
In Your strength
Guide me to the next steps
Though the waves
That try to flip over my kayak
For the memories
And my knowledge
Come from You
May my wisdom grow
Through each experience
That confronts me
So that I may
Better pave the way
For your return
Lead me
Day by day
To bring more people
To Your salvation
Help me to plant
The seeds of life
To further others in life
Come Lord
Quickly and swiftly

EXPECTATIONS

We live life in constant view
Of expectations
Whether they be of ourselves
Or of others
I do not see them as a burden
But an opportunity
To see things differently
I see them as a way
To transform yourself
Cause if you don't try different things
In life
How do you grow
In life
If you fail
At someone else's expectations
Don't beat yourself up
And grow resentful
Take it as a learning experience
And dust yourself off
For what works for one person
May not for another
But to try to reach
Someone else's expectations
Might give you the wisdom you need
To proceed in life
For every expectation you succeed at
Fulfills a new path

Of enlightenment
So, no
Not setting expectations
On yourself
Can be more negative
Than positive
Setting them on others
Can distill
What that person needs
To succeed
To move forward
But do not bring a person down
When they fail
In return
Show them much love
Give them a hand
And help them up
For expectations
Are only a blue print
Of chances to grow

GOD, THE WOMAN, AND ME

The stars remind me of home
I look up
Wanting to lay my head
Down upon the pillows
Laying down
Next to the woman of my life
The journeys Jesus put us on
Gave us purpose
Only drawing us closer
To one another
The memories
When we used to fly down
And do God's will
Remembering
Too many centuries
Of coming and going
To Earth
To come back
To holding each other
And the conversations
Were serene
Bringing healing
To each other's burdens
Over time
My anger got the best of me
My relationship with Jesus
Began to struggle
With the constant reminder
Of what I did

Therefore
My relationship with my wife
Began to struggle
When I was not angry
Because of my shame
The circumstances changed
And our relationship was quite pleasant
Love went all around the house
The beauty of heaven
And God's glory
Can't be explained
In words
For I have spent centuries
Building up
The riches of heaven
And doing God's will
Not to throw away
What He has given me
Everything!
The memories remain
Of the woman
Who is my wife
And the love
God has shown the both of us
For we are nothing
Without God

LOVE BEYOND LIFE

I begin to struggle
With my past
The struggles of war games
And the loss of life
My journey is a hard road
Just trying to remember the pieces
To fix the pot holes
Trying to remember
And piece back memories
The insanity creeps into me
To try to defeat me
Many men died
On the battlefield
Why do I still stand
Why do I have to remember
The men who died
Under my command
For I am ashamed
For their loss and their families
These people are heroes to me
I am their lost leader
Trying to hold onto their memory
I have stored them into my thoughts
To remember their legacy
For there is a quote
It is
"Death to the wicked."
For we all die
So does that mean
We are all wicked

It doesn't matter
At this point
Cause my heart
Is filled with grief
To those who have fallen
They have gone
Back to the ground
Which we come from
Onto the journey
Of their next home
Life is precious
Do not throw it away
Live each day
Like it is your last
For soldiers that die
Keep the peace in the world
The soldiers that are alive
Are known as Peacekeepers
And continue on their legacy
So I keep them in my memory
So that I may still show them love
Beyond life

THE URGE

I look down and see
A glass half full
What means more to me
The oxygen
Or liquor at the bottom
One gives life
The other brings death
So to soak my tongue
Could be the end of this man
For it has put me through jail
Institutions
And even death
The one thing
Calling out to me
That is not Jesus
I can't have
My body is hungry for more
But I can't give it
That satisfaction
For it will bring me back down
That downward spiral
The longing
To numb these emotions
Is bestowed upon my mind
The flood gates opened
And poured every emotion
Ten fold back into my life

Sometimes
It is too much of a burden for me
I try to rationalize myself
Into thinking I can use
Soak my nerves
With that poison
To think
I will become myself again
I don't want to become that person
Again
I then express my emotions
My shame
My self pity
My fears
My hurt and my anger
Sometimes though
The emotions take over
My whole day
But what I really need
Is a dose of Jesus Christ
To bring healing
And my urge to use will vanish
And be extinguished
From my mind

LASTING RELATIONSHIPS

There is nothing
Like a long lasting relationship
With a friend
Beginning to end
You are inseparable
All the events
Through the trials of life together
When the times get tough
It is not best to be on your own
They are always there
Giving out advice
And making compromises
For each other
When you are mad at each other
You work it out
Not hiding away
Out of fear
But it does happen
From time to time
Love goes both ways
And sometimes
You must be patient
With each other
When you are away
You miss each other

But just remember
I am only a phone call away
Call me with your problems
I want to hear them
So that I might open up
With what I struggle with in life
For there is always
Unconditional love
In these relationships
They seem more like family
Than a friend
Why would you want
To ruin such a great thing
As being a great friend to someone
Over disagreeing with them
So it is best
In the end
To make simple compromises
To make the relationship last

FATHER

Always try to keep things simple
For to be scatter-minded
Can bring you to a place
Of hopelessness
God's word cuts deep
Into the hearts of the simple minded
For I took time to be still
And be in His presence
To exalt Him
To get to know Him
Drawing close to Him
And the war of my mind
Has become calm
For the devil has fled from God
For God has a purpose
For me to fulfill
So I can't be a defeated child
While I am standing close to Him
I find myself
When I don't know what to do
I ask for His wisdom and knowledge
So that my steps are paved
To do His will
I sometimes find it hard
To be still
Cause I get caught up
In my pride
And decide to do my will
Over His

So I pray
Continually
So that I don't waver
From His path
For I am asking right now
What is the next door to walk through
To get me closer to You
For I am Your child
And You are my Father
I thank You for naming me
Your beloved
So I must have faith
In your judgement
And trust in your guidance
For I want what everyone wants
And that is love
I want there to be hope
That I have a future with You
So forgive me for doubt
Because You are my Father
And You are always with me

BRING ME OUT OF THE WILDERNESS

I am pushing myself
Toward the clouds
As I wander
Through the wilderness
This world beats me down
I am longing to go home
Now is not the time for that yet
So I wander
With a dry mouth and lips
Waiting for that cleansing water
To bring life back to me
So what do I do
With these burdens
That fill my mind
Hurting my soul
For I am crying out
For help inside myself
A longing
A need
To draw close to my Father
I walk
And see the light
At the end of the tunnel
The light draws me out of the darkness
Into God's glory
For He is always present
Where problems arise

And at every moment of my life
I need You
To guide me back home
So that I can walk with You
And see You face to face
And smile again
For all that I face in life
You have become my lighthouse
Showing me the way
Working out the good
And the bad
To do Your will
To fulfill what You need from me
Where do I go next
What do You need from me today, Lord
For though I wander
Through the wilderness
Still make Your presence known to me
Lead this worn out soul
To what You want me to be
Reveal to me
What You want from me
So that I can be close to You
So that I can be lead out
Of this wilderness

TO FILL A VOID

I write these words
To fill a void
In hope of a future
With my significant other
I feel I am voided out right now
It irks me
I ask
Why am I the one
Who is hurting
It is cause of my faults
And my mistakes
All I want
Is to love you
Be there for you
Help you amongst your struggles
You are always on my mind
It is a little annoying
But thank you
For everything
You have helped me with
I know you felt I did too much
But I was willing
To go the distance
With a willing heart
To help
And to use God's guidance
To guide you to the next steps in life
I am proud of you
For everything you accomplished
In the time I have known you

You had some set backs
Now it is time
For you to become
The woman you were meant to be
I would like
To keep in touch
And I hope
Your anger will recede
And we can work things out
I hope to talk to you soon
And even possibly hangout
It would bring me much joy
But to know
You are doing just fine
Puts a smile on my face
Also thank God
For the people God put in your life
That have influenced you
Also
Don't lose hope
But stay strong
Stay wise
And in wisdom and knowledge

WHEN YOU TELL GOD NO

This was the fall of a brother
2 angels come
And God seeks audience with me
I say
"No"
I don't want
To see His face right now
My anger and pride
Got the best of me that day
Cause me and 2 angels
Began to fight
To bring me to stand
Before Jesus Christ
My beacon goes off
As I see my wife and brother
On their bike
The battle closes in
Drawing closer to them
My heart races with fear
As I see the cause of the crash
About to happen
I seem them fly throughout the air
I catch my wife
And miss her brother
I place her on her feet
And apologize for her loss
I watched a great man die today
One I was proud to call brother
I took my leave
And went to heaven
With the 2 angels
I stood before God

Angry and lost
At what just happened
I was not hearing
What He had to say
And in my anger
I took a swing
God put me in my spot
Real fast
He pushes me
Towards the edge of clouds
I push away from the edge
And I seek forgiveness
Then I was thrown back
Into my human self
My heart
Spirit
Soul
Has changed since then
Cause I go to God
With all areas of my life
Wishing I could take that day back
That day of sorrow
And regret
That I told God
"No"

BEING LED BY CHRIST

The day has come
For me to be a shepherd
And lead my sheep to green pastures
Through God's glory
For I can hear His voice calling to me
Regardless of my faults
And regrets
He calls me as I am
Lead me to where You want me to go
Touching people along the way
To lead them back home
Let Your presence overflow
Throughout the world
As far East as also West
For Your presence is never ending
Take control
May Your words
Pierce the hearts of others
Through me
Take these words
On these pages
And touch many
So that they may learn
From my failures
As well as my successes
I write these words
According to God's will
He is longing for us
Every second of the day
Calling each of our names
To be sanctified

By Jesus Christ's blood
We then become purified
And cleansed of our sin
He is leading us toward a future
Hope
And everlasting life
So let's turn to Him
No matter where we are at in life
Become renewed in our soul
May He bear witness to us all
Through His spirit
For this is just the beginning
Of the blessing He has for us
Take over our lives
Forever and ever
Amen

COMPREHENSION

Comprehending my mistakes
Can be a great tool
For when the pieces of life
Fall apart
You now know whose fault it is
For to blame God
For the choices we have embraced
Is meaningless
Cause we got a glimpse of reality
It's futile to blame others
But you learn
From your part of the problem
Sometimes
It might leave you broken hearted
Left in complete brokenness
Not knowing what to do
With yourself
How do I fix what is broken
For time has come
For sorrow and grief
Two words I hate
Yet I can't get away from them
It has been a long hard road
Just to get stuck in my emotions
To create this hell
That seem to overtake me at times
Am I standing on the fence
To decide my fate

Which will I choose to push for
Heaven or hell
For I know heaven is home
And miss it everyday
So with what strength I have left
I turn to Jesus Christ
For I know I am nothing
Without His presence in my life
He takes me
And my burdens
That eat away at my soul
And takes them
And turns them into blessings
For what looks like a curse now
Might be the outlook
To move with purpose
To expose the truth to you
So don't let your hardships
Run you into the ground
But let them be a stepping stone
To a better life
Amen

MY DREAM IN TIME

Anger overtook me today
Cause I didn't get what I wanted
It appeared as a roaring lion
I took some of it out on a friend
I just wanted to get my book up
And ready to publish
For this is a dream I have
To inspire
Through a work of art called words
I had a talk with my mother
And she convinced me to look closer
Not from another state
So I can sit and
Watch the dream happen
Face to face
Plus the way life is right now
I must be patient
And in due time
A dream
Will become a reality
The overflow of treatment bills
Insurance
And car problems
I am faced with right now
Should I really add on another bill
As of right now
For I know I am ready
But is God done with this book
Will it ever be ready

I am deciding to be patient
And trust in God
Another question
Pops into my mind
Does God feel
I am good to go
I believe there is a plan here
Rather than staying in my anger
So I must look
And ask myself questions
Cause if I stay in my anger
I am being selfish
For all things will come
When purpose is exposed
And it will come to light in time

ASSASSIN

I blend in
In the wide open
I use stealth
To sheathe my blade
Opportunities arise
To take the kill
I am hunting
The most dangerous predator
Mankind
My thoughts linger
As my orders are given
Who is next
For what purpose
Does this man
Deserve to die
The differences between
Templars and assassins
The way to calm my thoughts
Is to save the innocent
May their flesh
Not touch my blade
For it is not in my instinct
To put away the tools
I have learned
From the brotherhood
Sometimes I wonder
What God's purpose is
In all this
For man kills man
With reason

I use my surroundings to move in
And stalk my prey
Who is deceived in his ways
I pull out my blade
And stab him in his back
My target falls to the ground
Laying in his blood
I speak
To get the info I needed
As he takes his last breath
I pray for him
And shut his eyes
With my target down
I disappear
Into the crowds
Running
Climbing
And hiding
From those that now hunt me
To escape I return
To my hideout
And turn back to my normal self
Till next time

FEAR FOR YOU

Not the way I want
To end my night
To get angry
Cause I am thinking of you
Pain strikes me
Cause I know I scared you away
Was not my intention to
How do you take what is going on
In the supernatural
And explain it to someone
In the physical realm
And expect them to be alright with it
It scares me to
But I am doing alright with it
I am as well as I can be
It's funny
My fear right now
Involves you
And you not talking to me again
Scared to let go of you
I just need to be strong
And let God do God in this
And I believe
We are going to talk again
It hurts though
To think and care
About someone so much
It drives you crazy

It sucks
I feel so stupid
To tell you the truths of life
And it blows up in my face
It puts a smile on my face
Cause I get a little relief
From telling you
There is hardship
That comes with certain realities
I will face my fears one day
And I hope to make amends with you
In the future
For now
I can go to bed
With a smile on my face
And know you are ok
Don't let the truth hurt you
But accept who you are

A BLESSED DAY

Today was a God day
Today was a day
To get out of myself
And reach out to people
I was a friend to someone
That needed to get the monkey
Off his back
I played treasurer
At the noon meeting
I got to be a speaker at a meeting
And see my sponsor
I got a blessing from a friend
And good advice on my book
I see more as prophecy
Of what he spoke to me
I got to go to another meeting
Where I heard a man speak of his life
As hard as his life is
He taught me not to give up
I went to Ham Lake Lanes
Where I enjoyed
Fellowship and food
And got to see people
I haven't seen in years
I also took time out of my day
To draw close to God
Who I owe this day to

Thank you, Lord
For opening opportunity
To push forward
Thank You
For all the people
You brought into my life today
For each person was a blessing
And an inspiration
To stay clean
And live a sober life
So, Lord
I ask
Let there be more days
Like today
More opportunities to grow
And bring me closer
To Your likeness
For today
And everyday
Even the hard days
I give the Lord
Gratitude and praise

PRAISE IN TROUBLED TIMES

As time presses
Against the longevity of life
I see my problems
More and more clearly
A sixth sense arises within me
Revealing the truth of who I am
There are those
Who want to rise against me
Bring me down
To a standard of life
That is not me
I bow down
To pick the pieces of the puzzle
Back up
So that I can fit
The pieces back together
For I know I can't do this
By myself
Self-will is not enough
At this point in my life
I need that spiritual food
To fill me up
And take me out
Of my despair
For when pressed against a wall
And cornered
It feels like the world
Weighs me down
Who is this tyrant
I have become

I know I am not a monster
Because I have the heart
And soul
Of an angel
Which means God
Is always there
Guiding me
To the road to heaven
As long as I am on Earth
I will live
And face my problems
On God's terms
For He is my stepping stone
The rock of my salvation
The pieces come together
As He wills
For my purpose
Step by step
My pleasure
Is knowing You are there
For my struggles today
Become my strengths tomorrow
For all honor is from God
Through His glory
May my faith illuminate
Who You are to the world
Lord
You deserve
The praise of everyone
Restore joy to those I love
Today and forever
Amen

CRY OUT TO JESUS

There is a time
Not to fear your circumstances
A time to stand up
And be courageous
And not let fear entice our lives
For fear can be like a virus
Spreading through our flesh
Cause us to be paralyzed
With our steps of faith
But we can always
Cry out for Jesus
For He is always with us
Do not let the hammer
Crush your foundation
Into dust
Fears runs away
When we turn
To our Father in heaven
For when God is near
Who can be against us
Troubled are the ones
Who lack faith
And allow fear
To run their lives
For each step of faith
Do not become weary
But if it does happen
And doubt takes control
Cry out to Jesus Christ
For we are His children
And He keeps close to us
Ever present

At every moment
Live in His love for you
It is everlasting
And paid with by His blood
For all love chases away fear
I try to linger in this though
Cause I do not always
Feel loved
I don't want to be stuck
With fear running my life
So I then turn the other cheek
And run toward love
How do I do this
I cry out to Jesus Christ
My Lord and Savior

CHAOTIC LOVE

The mysteries
Of the concept of thievery
To take what is not yours
For your own benefit
It is a hurtful
Humiliating way
To bring someone down
The fear it embeds
Into the heart of man
The joy of life stolen
In a moment's notice
The hard work
Put into what is lost
Seems futile
Cause of greed
Should we have to suffer
I hope not
Because
Regardless of our hardships
I can still find hope
That this thief can change
Into a new creation
I find anger
But I find myself
Wanting to forgive
Whoever did this to us
If it is someone I know
I would pay them a visit
Regardless of feelings
So that I may encourage them
To change
Cause as much as I want
Revenge

It is always the time
To show love
Whether they want it or not
I have a feeling
A hard time is coming to you
So why not be there
To pick them up
It can be a time of
Renewal
And healing
Between them and I
For this
Is a shitty situation
That can be voided out
Through love
Just show up
And may their heart change
Right in front of you
Watch good from bad
And watch
How someone's life is changed

OH, LORD

Here I stand
Waiting for confirmation
Waiting for my calling
To be fulfilled
Looking for the path
Laid out for me
I ask that my path
Comes to light to me
So that I can follow You
Sufficiently
Sometimes I feel
I have the blinders on
And tend to wander
Waywardly
Draw me closer to You
Oh, Lord
So that I may see
The footsteps I am to walk
More clearly
Some people
See my way of thinking
As false
I see
That I am just more aware
I am the way I am
Because of the wisdom
You instilled in me
Which is not the normal way of thinking
Anointed
I walk in Your glory
My life is where You want me

Where do I go today
To bring light into the world
May darkness fade
As You light the way
Keep my attitude on Your ways
And not my own
Bless those who come my way
Through Your presence
And help me to help them
Where they are at
For today is what I have
May I bask in it with You
As You change me
Into what You want
To fulfill Your purposes
In this life
I change for You
Oh, Lord
For to change for You
Is to change for myself
Draw me closer to You
Oh, Lord
That everything
Becomes for You

RIDICULED FOR FAITH

My purpose is proposed
To make the way
Of the coming of Jesus Christ
People are going to try
To persuade me not to
But I must stand firm
In the task
In which God has purposed to me
I know
Much ridicule is to come
As my journey progresses
I know
People are going to state
That I am crazy
For I know
This is the persecution
Which people before me
Went through
The bible shows me
A glimpse
Of what may come to me
But I must count all circumstances
As a time to give God praise
And count it all joy
I am finding myself
Right now
In times of turmoil
Where some people
Are looking at me crazy
Saying that all this
Is just a part of mental illness
I think not
If it is so

Study my brain
I have real
Out of body experiences
And receive
Real visions from the Lord
I don't know a medication
That can change my mind
About what the Lord does
Through me and in me
Normal is kinda lame
To me
Sometimes it seems so futile
Living a spiritual life
Things keep progressing
In the plan
In which Christ wills
Which brings more joy to my life
So a little bit of persecution
To help you grow
In your faith
Will help in the coming trials
To come and stand firm
In the foundation
Which Christ built for you

GRASS

I look into the looking glass
There is an image
That needs to be decoded
And interpreted
To those it is for
I look to see
The black blisters of grass
Wave
From side to side
Not knowing
Which way to go
I watch as a man
Calms the winds
And everything comes to rest
And be still
In His presence
In His hand
He holds a rake
Like a staff
He starts to rake the grass
Separating
The dead from the living
The dead grass He rakes up
And is thrown into bags
And thrown away
The living grass
Is then tended to
Fertilized
And grows and grows
He then aerates the ground
And gives breath
To the grass

Renewing
And nourishing to health
In due time
The lawn must be mowed
This is the time
To cut out the good
From the bad
For when we grow
We might also
Welcome back things
Which keep us from growing
So they must be cut off
And thrown away
So that we may grow
More and more
For when the man takes care
Of each sliver of grass
As a child
To give it light and rest
When we are still
And allow Him to take care of us
For you can never be separated
From His love

CHANGING TIDES

The tide turns
As time passes
I watch
As the moon eclipses
It turns
To the color of blood
As time draws near
I feel
The tears of blood
Drip from my eyes
Is this
My turning point
I look up
To catch my breath
For I felt my heart stop
For a moment
Does it all mean
My time is near
Am I going to have
A tyranny on myself
At this point
I yell out
Parlay
Which then
I can make a treaty
With God
To save this wretch
For right now
I am scared
Of what is new to me
But I love it
Because it is unknowing

For this is my blessing
And disguise
To go forth in obedience
And see where You lead me
Unknowing
What trials You place before me
And to praise You
With every step I take
For my waywardness
Brought me
To my own demise
I fell
Cause I clung
To disaster
Which overtook my sanity
Putting me
Into that place of humiliation
So that I could
Get a hold of humility
So I could become humble
In my actions
For my fall
Became my time to rise up
I clung
To what I knew was true
And changed my attitude
And outlook
From God's grace
My faith keeps me humble
To His voice
Listen and look for who you are
In Jesus
Nowhere else
For when your eyes are on Him
And you are seeking
The truth will set you free

MY FRUSTRATIONS AND HOW I DEAL WITH OTHERS

Sometimes it feels like
People come to me
When they want something
The moment I give a helping hand
I feel like
I get left in the dust
It is not like that
With all people though
I love to help
But I feel people use my kindness
Against me
I don't like to watch
The suffering of others
I put myself out there
So that God
Can ease their suffering
Through myself
Sometimes I feel it is a burden
Cause I have to decide
When I should give to others
Plus allowing God
To fulfill my needs as well
For I never want
To be selfish
Cause I have to know
When to say no
Hoping I am not missing
The curve ball
That is thrown to me
For if I can help everyone

I would
This concept
Tends to frustrate me
For I know
During these situations
I must bring it to God
To evade my enemies
Attacks of self-worth
What I do love
Is that people do come to me
With their problems
And God opens the door
For me to be there
For someone in need
Why does He use me this way
There is only one explanation
And that is cause He can
So out of this
I thank God
For the struggles
That come my way
So that I may grow
And others also

CHANGES FROM A GODLY HEART

Today is a day
To make changes for the better
The day to lessen
My expectations of others
And to come to them
As I am
For this
Is a new way of life for me
So I am to work
On my defects of character
And my shortcomings
For I know I fall short
Of God's glory
Everyday
Day by day
I reconcile my faults to God
For the issues
That come to me
Are there to push me forward
In my faith
To paint that picture
Of healing
Renew me
Into the person
He wants me to be
I find sometimes
The whirlwind in my head
Sounds like static
Making it hard to hear You
When this happens
Your spirit still guides my soul

Step by step
Till I can hear You
And the static stops
For I know You do not forsake
And leave us
You are always present
In every circumstance
For the changes I have made
Do not come
From my own selfish desires
But they come
From my reliance on You
For when You are in control
Your will for me is exposed
So let my desires
Line up with Yours
Allowing me to live
More and more like You
For a Godly heart
Will change the world

LOOKING FOR LOVE

What happens when the tides turn
And your cards run out
This is my bleeding heart
My circumference
To my sorrow
Wanting
But not receiving
All I have
Is a bunch of what if's
I cry out
For I am lonely
I long for companionship
Should I make a little compromise
To fill what I don't have
Just to lie alone
Wishing there was someone
Next to me
I miss it
Cause the joy
Of not being alone
Causes me to strive
It beckons at my soul
To love someone
More and more
I should not try
To fill the void through lust
But I find myself
Reaching out for it
When I do
I miss my opportunity
To love myself more

I beat myself down
With my internal emotions
For I know
There is hope
And I know
That love
Will find itself to my feet
For when it does
My path will be clear
To love the woman
Who will be at the end of the line
Standing there
Waiting for me to arrive
To take her into my arms
To be more submissive
To each other
For this is my struggle
Right now
For I know God will lead her to me
In hope of telling
Our love story

4TH TO THE 5TH STEP

Today I am at the finish line
Of the step
That I am working on
I came to the conclusion
That I am being a sloth
And procrastinating
So I sat down
To sit down
And finish my 4th step
I can tell I am going
To get a lot out
When I go on to step 5
I am scared
Cause I got to do it
With both my sponsors
This is my moment
An opportunity
To let go and let God
Move through me
And to get my story out
To other people
That are struggling
Like myself
I might be
Letting my fears
Get the best of me
So I must do this
To gain my freedom
And break the chains of bondage
That are keeping me

From progressing forward
I want to thank everyone
But most importantly, God
For bringing me
To this breaking point
For now
Is the time to take action
And walk the straight path of life
Pushing through my fears
Step by step
To become free
Cleaning the house
Throwing away the junk
This is my renewing of mind
Body
And soul
Bring me to the point
Bring me
To the 5th Step

LET'S WORK IT OUT

This frustration
Is killing me inside
At one moment we were so close
Yet in an instant
You won't talk to me
I feel thrown to the dirt
And like I was left to die
My resentment only grows
As you sit silent
I just wish
To work out the issue
For someone you said you cared about
At one point
Now you can't even take the time
For me to explain
What is going on with me
It is pissing me off
That you are bringing in
The rest of your family
Over an issue
With me
Let us sit
And work out the issue
You and I
And let's not let fear
Hold us back
And make amends
I still want you
To be a part of my life

How can I fix
What is shattered
How can I pick up the pieces
And put the pieces back together
If you don't let me
I kinda find it funny
In a way
That out of all the issues
In this world
That you
Are my biggest issue
You are the issue
I want to confront
More than the rest of them
It did bring me much joy
To hang with your mom
And all the siblings
And watch a movie
Would have been cooler
If you were there
I do apologize
For putting this on Facebook
But there is no other way
To get a hold of you
And I know you read my writings
So can you make time
So we can work out
Our issues

ALIGNING THE SOUL

The letting go of the self
The release of your life
Into God's hands
So He can piece you
Back together again
According to His purpose
To have vision
To open your eyes
To see His purpose
Aligning yourself to His will
Growing in the fruits of the spirit
He bears witness to me
For I pray
For my heart of stone
To be removed
And replaced
With a heart of flesh
For I feel
My human body and spirit
Live
Two totally different lives
Going
Two totally different directions
That lead to the purpose
Which I am created for
How can a part of you
Go one direction
And the other
The other direction
The answer
Is in the miracle of Christ, Jesus
Sometimes this seems
Like an optical illusion

But the reality is that
His ways
Are beyond my understanding
So in order to have the knowledge
To understand
Is to ask
And He will show you
What you can handle
Through what you see
And what you are told
You are then able
To speak prophecy
Into the world around you
Don't do what I did
And try to run away
Because God
Is everywhere
So eventually
You just run back
Into His arms
With His acceptance of you
And He surrounds you
With love

WHAT IF

Who is trying
To pull the strings
To play the puppet master
Who will represent our country
In South Korea
To make the way
To pave the path
For freedom
For there are those
Who threaten
Our way of life
And the life of others
The compelling story
Of allies and axis
Confronting each other
Through action
We stand ready
Prepared
For the worst
How do we build relations
Between the North and South
The answer lies
In the knowledge
Of histories past
For they were once one
And not divided
To possibly be pulled
To the brink of war
Breaks my heart
For it longs for peace
Among the nations
With each threat
It draws closer and closer
Opening the door
For an early grave

I would stand up
For our country
And it's values
I would love
To sit and strategize
What the outcome can be
But the truth is
What is the logical solution
To the divided Korea's
For sanctions seem to work
For a while
Till they need more money
So they break the sanctions
To extort money
We can't let them
Keep extorting
So no matter what
Tell them
"No"
Cause at the worst
Treaties are broken
And start of war begins
I would take the position
That no one wants
To do my countries biddings
As Ambassador of the South
To do all I can
To keep the peace
May God bless you all
For God has blessed America

CORRUPTION OF THE TONGUE

The feeling you get
When you think something is funny
In your mind
And state it
Just to end up
Offending someone
The discomfort
Of feeling guilt and shame
Knowing what you said
Was wrong
To approach them
To right what was wrong
And to admit your fault
Places you
In a state of vulnerability
It puts you in the spotlight
And fear seems to trickle
Into my flesh
For I wait for the outcome
To put yourself in this position
Is never pleasing
For it could have been avoided
By not pulling out
My whip and lashing tongue
Sometimes the best thing you can do
Is shut your mouth
Sometimes it changes the events to come
For words can kill a man's soul
And they can last forever

In this life
For what I say
Affects everyone
Who is around to hear
The information
Which can change or kill a person
Soften my heart
Soul
And mind
That I may renew myself
That my words bring healing
To a person
Not condemnation
For I wish to bring
Joy and love
Not anger and hurt
To people
For to remember
That the words I say
Affect everyone around me
And let me speak life
Not death

A PRESSING MOMENT

A moment of peace
Flows through me
As I release my secrets
Kept away
From the one I love
In hope of restoration
Of our relationship
Which has faltered
I have allowed fear of rejection
To cloud my mind
And of what she might think of me
Tonight
A step was taken
Of courage
To tell her
Some of my secrets
What she does with them
Is out of my control
But I take that fear
And give it to God
For God is my strength
And refuge
Knowing He
Is going to protect me
And use this for His purpose
In my life
To fulfill His will
In and through me
It has been a long time coming
I tried to get her to sit down
And talk
So I had to do it publicly
Which was not the way

I wished to do it
But I prayed
And I believed
That God was leading me to
So I did
And released some of the burden
That I was holding back
My love goes out
Unconditionally to her
I will have to accept
What happens from here is good
Is it bad
I do know
That God has me
Regardless of what happens
So blessed be her heart
And take into perspective
Of where I am coming from
So that we may restore
What was a good relationship

THE RENEWING

I look into the soul
Of a mirror image of myself
I then ask myself
Where did my joy go
Where is the hope
I once had
Darkness
Seems to cloud my memories
I look closer to see
A glimmer of hope
Still in my heart
That glimmer of God
Is the very thing
That is keeping me going
Right now
Giving me the strength to continue
To progress further
In my faith
For I know
I don't deserve Your grace
But it was a gift
Given through Your mercy
And through the death
Of Your son, Jesus Christ
I feel lost in complex situation
One which brings much fear
A fear that is dragging me
Down a lonely road
Dragging
My thoughts and actions
Into a darkness
That can only be brought through
To shine all my weaknesses
So I ask
Let my soul shine again

And bask in Your glory
I now see my soul begin to shake
And blood drip from the heavens
Covering my soul
I see a chalice
With living water
Poured over me
To cleanse the blood
And the darkness
That has been running rampant
Through my soul
Another day
A renewing of oneself
Through the blood and water
Of Jesus Christ
Through You I am renewed
Let me now live in Your ways
And in Your presence always
Amen

SINKING SAND

Bewilderment
Collides with ambition
Reacting
In a chaotic downward spiral
Anxious to get back up
But all I can do
Is sit up
It is as if
I am in sinking sand
Struggling
With my reality
Struggling
With the thought
Of this is it
Am I able to pull myself out
I scream for help
And I feel
No one is listening
This loneliness
Clouds my thought
With negativity
Is this my judgement day
Will this be the day
My lungs stop working
And heart pounding
As I release my last breath
At this point
The sand is over my head
All you can see of me
Is a wrist and hand
Waiting to be gripped
To be pulled out
Of the miry sands
That seem to close in
On my soul

I have lost all hope
At this point
Then
Within a moment
I feel someone
Grip my hand
Hope starts to flicker again
As my head
Reaches the surface
My heart and lungs
Start to pound
As breath releases
From my lips
I now am on solid ground
And give praise
To the one who saved me
He calls me child
And hugs me
And puts me on my feet
He takes my hand
and walks me to safety
And tells me
I have been save by grace
And have faith
for I am with you
So I call Him by name
and say thank You
Jesus

LETTER TO GOD

I am tempted
To travel to the land
In which God
Will eventually put my feet
Will I go to waste away
In the desert
Will my journey take me to Chicago
Before I go
I am excited to see
What God will do through me
Cause I know His blessing is upon me
I know there will be much hardship
But I do know
That I will flourish
If I stand strong in my faith
Let me see Your will for me
More clearly every day
I am not running
But waiting patiently
On Your timing
I am trying to see
Your will more clearly
So I can become
More obedient to Your purposes
I wish not to be rushed
Into the possibility of death
So I wait
For the signs of Your calling
I will be diligent
To progress in my walk with You
To create the history

You foretold through prophecy
To attempt the impossible
Through Your presence
And power guiding me through
By the Holy Spirit
For I have hope
That I will walk and talk with You, Jesus
Face to face again
And be able to come home
Forgive me for my complications
I have created
Let us come together
So that I may do Your work

STARING INTO FEAR

There is fear
Trying to learn
From my instability
I look and see this reality
Not just in the physical
But I look into
The spiritual realms as well
Some say I am delusional
Others say I need help
Which people
Am I more prone to accept
For there are past instances
That I know
What did happen
And I am sick
Of being told
That none of it was true
I am sunken
By what I hide
For what I tell you
Is only a little bit
Of my struggle
I hate to hide
Because I am not hiding well
My inner struggles
Are real
And they build up
Till I have no choice
But to release them
In the world
I do not tell my story
To scare you
But I tell it
So that you may learn
A thing or two

For a compelling gesture
Put yourself in my shoes
What don't I tell you
What is the battle
That rages within
It is a complex situation
And pieces seem scrambled
I am also looking for answers
Looking for the clues
To piece me back together
I am looking for stability
In an unstable world
For when Normal
And Abnormal
Are both chaotic
Which one seems more fitting
To progress yourself in this life
For these
Are some of my fears
That give me a haunting glare
While I search for the truth
Of who I am

A LITTLE PRAYER

What am I not seeing, Lord
I would like
To see this situation
From Your eyes
I no longer have control
And am losing myself
Over such a matter
How I long for answers
How I long for Your counsel
I feel like
I am just a burden right now
Reveal to me
The solution to my problem
So I can move forward
I want to let it go
But I feel so consumed by it
What do I do
It is like pressing a pressure point
And not releasing
A little bit
Like being shot in the heart
I know You can use this
To better me
Why do I have so much love
For someone
Who doesn't love me
For God put that love there
For a reason
I don't know why now

So I doubt and wonder
Why You put her in my life
In the first place
What is this all for, Lord
I beckon to know
Where will You take me from here
And will I ever see her again
I am angry and sad
Please bring healing and comfort
To this torn soul
Help me and release me
From this burden
For this is a bad story
Of the beauty
And the beast
May your love complete me, Lord
Amen

BENGHAZI

My name is David O'Meara and this is a dream I had revolving around the Benghazi attack September 11, 2012. (Actually, the night of.)

It started off with me surrounded by terrorists. Them listening as I gave out the plans. We were to capture Stevens at the consulate and mortar attacks and full frontal assault. Later that evening we then started our march toward the consulate. I asked one of the terrorists to go and recruit more people. And as we drew closer some of the men started to fire their weapons into the air. I stayed outside as a man came up the street and started firing. After a couple of bazooka shots and some Molotovs the building was on fire. I then periodically pull out my radio for military chatter and kept asking where are my men? Where are my men? This is getting out of hand.

A voice came over the radio with the stand down orders. I was so pissed. And a man with a bazooka ran by and I grabbed it and he fell to the ground. I took it and pointed at the consulate and fired. I watched it fly into and blow up, killing one of the navy seals that was with Stevens. I fell to my knees and was like 'No. This can't be happening. WTF?' then I watch Stevens being pulled from the building as they are beating him. I then watch him get stabbed. And right before he is about to kill him, I wrestle the guys off of him and walk him to his car, gun pointed ready to shoot. I put him in the car and one of the terrorists orders two of them to go with us.

I start driving and Stevens starts talking and one terrorist tells him to shup up and stabs him in the jugular. I freak out and he says he is just an American anyways. I ask him are you a recruit or one of the originals in the group. He says he just wanted to kill Americans. So I pull out my gun and shot him in the face. I slam on the breaks and look at the other passenger. I tell him I am American and shot him in the face.

This all happened within two blocks. I then got out and pulled Stevens from the car and pulled him out in front of the car. He then speaks to me and tells me this all happened cause of you. As I watch him take his last breath and watch the life fade from his eyes. I start to cry and two more terrorists walk up and say he was just American. I shot one and the other gets the shot off. I then shot to kill him. I get up, walk back to the consulate, and as they are running by me I start firing. Then one terrorist asks what are you

305

doing? I am American and fire and kill him. I keep firing till I have no ammo and they overwhelm me. They begin to stab me over and over. I lay there, spit blood, and a terrorist walks over with a rifle and shoots me in the face.

Next thing I know I am at the compound on the roof with the remainder of the soldiers that are left. They went over their plans to secure the compound. All of a sudden, I hear a boom and in my head I think to myself, here come the mortars. They begin to hit and I watch one of the soldiers fall to his knees and watch as his IBA catches him from falling over but he dies. A mortar hits and throws me and another soldier off the roof. I am on my knees crying for my failures that night that previous took place. I watch as the other soldier takes cover. I begin to leave the battlefield with my head in the ground. God begins to talk to me. And ask if I was going to help. I said I have failed you yet again.

I want you to help them. I got excited and my first action was to go after the mortars. I got there and slaughtered them all. Jim rigged the mortar cannon so that if anyone use it, it would blow up on them. Then I headed back to the compound to help with the waves of enemies coming. I saw a man trying to climb the wall one of the waves and I slit his throat and I looked up at one of the soldiers and told him I am here to help and I took care of the mortar cannons. Then in the background you hear a big boom in the background and I said you see. Wave after wave came and we made every bullet count. Toward the end I began to think to myself is this ever going to end. Then right before the sun came up, it was over. I then erased the memories of me ever being there.

Yes this is what I dreamt about on September 11, 2012. I woke up, went to work, and came home to hear about the Benghazi attack. This is my dream. This is my memory. How God sent an angel to help save who was left. If you can use this in your investigation, please do. I am sending this that it might fill in some blanks. If not hope you enjoyed. Just trying to help. This is just what I remember. Wish I could help further.

PUZZLED

Telling the story
Of the homemade puzzle
A work of art
Filling the space
Between time
And a way to fit in
This is the torch
Beneath my feet
The warmth
Creeping from my toes
To the edges of my hair
Can we all be put back together
Through the touch of the torch
Or will we burn
To be forgotten
There is a thought
That lingers within my heart
The answer is found within
Will I come to a point
To where I stand
Beside the ocean
As time tends to stand still
Have that moment of Zen
That freedom
In my mind
And soul
A time
When the puzzle pieces
Fall apart
Come together
To make me
Into a new person
Brought together
In a totally new way
But fitting the pieces

Together
Yet always come apart
And come back together
In a new form
This is the exercise
Of what life can give
But there is a blessing
Every time
Curve balls are thrown
Your way
For this is the evolution
That creates us anew
Ever changing
Ever growing
To blossom
Into the new picture
We become
Awaiting the outcome

THE STRUGGLE OF HER

Here I am stuck
Between
Letting go and holding on
Fears of the what ifs
Creep up
Emotions
Within my soul
What I want
I may never get
But the love I feel
For her is real
I don't want to forget her
But need to let go
For the time being
For my thoughts
Light the flame
Of emotions
An eagerness
To be a part of her life
For the words written were honest
And my struggle is real
I know I pushed her away
With honesty
And hurt her
To be that honest
And be that fragile
And tell her
What has been going on
Was freeing
But I find myself feeling sad
Cause of her lack of presence
Her presence always brought me joy
But I could tell
She struggled
And made me sad

When she would have
An empty smile
Trying to hide
That she was a mess
I had to tell her my secrets
That she might be able
To work on herself
The memories I hide
From her thoughts
To hide our secrets
Yes
Fear overwhelmed me
The outcome I expected
Now I miss her
With all my heart
Even though she is closer
Than she appears
My memories are not all good
And I get angry
To think about them
Those feelings show that I care
And I still love her
I say it
Every time I think of her
I wish she was here
So I can say it
And show her
How I feel about her

A BIG PRAYER

To be touched by an angel
Is a blessing from God
To feel again
Is unbearable at times
For God speaks to my heart
And bears witness
To the angel in me
The mind is a timid place
And can create the chaos
Which appears in our lives
What is your perception
How do you perceive things
I try to think of things
To store in heaven
My mind
Can take a turn for the worst
And lead me astray
In my heart
The word is living
And pulling to the unknown
Closer to the world of God
He has put me in charge
Of angels
To do His will
And fulfill His purpose
Lead me God
Through the guidance
Of Your spirit
For I know I have been forgiven
Through Christ, Jesus
And He lives in me
Use me
Oh Lord
In the manner You deem necessary
I know the journey is long

And comes with its burdens
So help me
To do things in Your timing
Help me
To accept the way things are
So I may better do Thy will
Change me inside out
Help me
To become more like You
Open my eyes
To see the spiritual
Amongst the physical
May I spread the love
You have shown me
Onto others
That I may better bear witness
To Your glory
Show me the path
Which You ask me
To bear my cross
And follow You
Amen

BLACK WATER

Here I walk
The desert of dismay
Surrounded by people
Who wish to kill me
Not knowing
Enemy from foe
We took on a contract
To fight this war
Not knowing
Who was enemy or foe
We took on the world
Face to face
With adversity
We shot
At everything that moved
Not thinking
Of the consequences
Not caring
About civilian life
We would soon find out
The consequences
Of our lack of order
And not following
The rules of war
Soon the people grew tired
If we were going to end their lives
So they fought back
They captured us
And beat us
Within an inch of our lives
Took a rope
And put it over a post
And hung us
Still alive
Kicking

And feeling life
Beginning to leave us
They continued to beat us
Hopelessness
Erupted in our being
As they light us on fire
The pain unbearable
As I pass out
Till I was dead
From lack of oxygen
I then awoke
From the dream
Went on with my day
And when I turned on the news
I saw
My dead body on fire
And they were still
Beating our bodies
This is my reality
Do I have
Out of body experiences
Or am I delusional
These are some of the things
I see while I sleep
I do struggle
With the mental aspect
Of life

MENTALLY PAVED

This is the battle
Of my mind
Trying to figure out
What is real
And what is delusion
Is this mental illness
Or is it something
Out of the normal
That God thinks
I can handle
For I know
God won't give me
More than I can handle
At a time
I know my struggle
Is real
But I know God is bigger
Than my struggle
So I tend to test the waters
But even that
Sometimes ruffles
The bystanders
So how
Do I get the help
I need
When no one wants to know
What I do
I don't say these things
To scare people
I do it
To open their minds
To a new perspective
Of my life
And the struggle within
Which I deal with

Day in
And day out
The steamroller
Trying to take me out
Of this life
For I know
Who can handle the situation
And He is working in me
And through me
To tell my story
My testimony
The story of love
For this sinner
Not worthy of grace
But is gifted with it
For this is the battle
For life and death
A ruling story
Of my travels
Through time and space
Moving
Pace to place
Each step paved
Before taken
For if God is for me
Who can be against me

ONWARD STRUGGLE

Being persuaded
In the direction
Of what's
At the end of the tunnel
Will I come out of the darkness
Unscathed
Or will I be a stronger person
Pushed to his limits
For I am sometimes lost
In my frailty
Will I learn
From the latter days
To improve my future
To blossom
To grow
Into something beautiful
For I don't want
To be lost
In my own demise
What brings on
This cripple effect
What is this emotion
Hitting me
Crashing over me
Trying to destroy
All the work I have done
I need to fear less
And love
The only thing
To lift up the broken
For turmoils
Come and go
Do I choose
To learn from each one
Or learn to resent

Who I am
For I know
My own forgiveness
Will begin
With the forgiveness of others
I am still learning
To accept myself
The way I am
Troubled
By the thoughts of hope
And dreams revealing
A path of life
That will not bring me harm
But what do I have to do
To achieve this luxury
This is sad
For sometimes I struggle
With purpose
But I long
To fulfill the gaps
To finish
The race of life

TRICKLED FEAR

This is my fall
To remember
The memories
Of my mistakes
To be succumbed
By the thoughts
Of what I have done
Beaten till broken
And shattered
To be brought back
To the dust in which I came
I feel the decay
Inside myself
The manure
Flung out into the sun
Left to dry
Till I end up
On someone's shoe
Being walked on
Over and over
I want this fear to end
The struggle is simple
But for a double-mind man
It becomes
The obstacle of life
With death
Staring you in the eye
Mocking your every move
How do I lift this shadow
That holds me inside
This darkness
I can't allow to take me
Down the road of despair
What treachery awaits me
I tend to wonder

As my anxiety grows
I feel weak in my knees
Maybe I should get on them
And pray
For this moment
My peace with everything
Is in disarray
I can't do this
On my own
So I found myself
Reaching out
But the memories
Drip
Fear
Like a trickle
Through my veins
I could have
The best day
Then at a moment's notice
It is taken
Help captive
By my fears
Draining me
To point to where
I have no other way
But to surrender
And turn to the one
That picks me up
And places me
On firm ground
The Son who died
And rose from the dead
Jesus Christ